may this book ⟨?⟩
God's love and

THIS PEOPLE.

The Creation Project

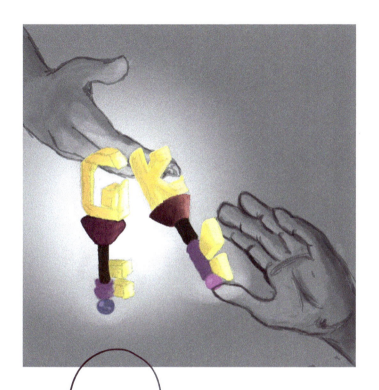

From the plan book of God

Of Sunshine

Written from the imagination of

Sunshine Rodgers

Illustrations by:
Travis Rodgers and Max Steele

RWG Publishing
PO Box 596
Litchfield, IL 62056
https://rwgpublishing.com/

Published in the United States of America

Paperback: 9781795588003

Hardcover: 978-0-359-39854-6

to my best friend, Travis

A note to my readers:

This is just a personal rendition of this Divine friendship and not to be taken as the Truth and the Word. Honestly, I wasn't there. I don't know all that happened. I am no expert on the beginning of literal time. All I know is that there was a world before this current world began a long long long time ago. I was able to pick up, the one you also keep somewhere close I'm sure, a copy of God's plan book. And as I read it, I get a sense that there was more to the story, more to the words and more to the action. Let's follow along together as we figure out piece by piece what could have happened up in Heaven all before Day 1 officially began.

- Sunshine

"Your heart became proud on account of your beauty, and you corrupted your wisdom because of your splendor."
– Ezekiel 28:17

Introduction

When I was asked to write the Forward to Sunshine's latest book, *The Creation Project,* I was so honored. First, because I have known her for at least a decade, and I know the quality of person that she continues to be. Second, because I know the depth of commitment that she has for her Lord and Savior Jesus Christ. Last, I know the amount of heart that she pours into every composition. Though I was honored, I still could not put my name on a book that I had not read - especially one that touched upon theological issues. As I read her book I found myself at odds with several deeply important theological concepts that were at that time between its pages. I knew I needed to have a conversation with Sunshine to see what was on her heart about what she wrote. I found her as brilliant as usual and highly sensitive to the things of God. It blessed the teacher side of my temperament to find her so teachable. As I voiced my concerns she took copious notes and asked poignant questions concerning the person of God and His attributes.

To be fair and honest, I had never really thought about the idea that God and Lucifer must have had a relationship before Lucifer was cast out of heaven. My mind was secure in the knowledge that the devil is bad, and God is good. I, like most Christians, know that Lucifer/Satan is a defeated foe and that he is "under our feet" because of Calvary's cross and Jesus's sacrifice for us. However, what happened before the fall of man? What happened before Lucifer and his angels' rebellion? As an evangelist with a Master of Divinity, my window of experience is narrowed to winning the lost with a focus on the cross and not necessarily about what it took to get humanity to this point (with the obvious exception of the Genesis account of the fall of man and the serpent's/Satan's roll in that event). So, when I read Sunshine's book, it was a scary recalibration of my thought process and a refreshing re-pondering of lifelong ideas.

In consideration of this manuscript, I had to come to some "givens." First, Sunshine is NOT a theologian. She is, however, a lover of God. Second, her aim was not to write a theological treatise on the person of God. If someone wants that, one will not find it in a one hundred page manuscript. One will find that in several volumes in a seminary library, and still, the sections will fall VERY short of who God really is. Third, this work's whole desire is to cause one to "feel" a little of what God felt on the day His creation fell and He found Himself at the place of casting Lucifer out of heaven. Fourth, Sunshine wants people to see God as good—to make Him approachable. It must have worked because when I shared Sunshine's manuscript with my daughter, she said, "Dad, it made me want to come to God. I saw Him as kind and approachable." Mission accomplished, Sunshine!

Are there things in this book that will bother some people? Of course, there are. That is true of just about any book these days. But stop and think about how anyone would communicate some of the deepest aspects of God's nature and person. The Trinity (God as three in one) is one of the most impossible things to discuss in theology. No matter how one tries to describe it, one falls short. Across denominational lines, people just see it all differently.

So with all this in mind let us see this work for what it is. It is a parable from the heart of a loving and courageous young woman who blends a little fiction into a real happening so that some may see the loving heart of her Mighty God. In this fiction, one will find how she portrays the relationships between the various persons of God framed in the real historical happening of the rebellion in heaven and the subsequent fall. This fiction is also found in how she depicts the angels in their building program and their outfits. However, who's to say that it was not that way? There is no one to bear witness to it.

So let us, therefore, enjoy Sunshine's vision, and do what one does with a parable—glean from it what spiritual truths one can. See the heart of God in it. Know that He adores you and I; and because He does, He came to us with a plan of salvation. Maybe Sunshine will come to that in her next book. I cannot wait to find out. Until then I invite you to open your heart, reject being critical, and enjoy *The Creation Project*!

Blessings,

Evangelist Carl B. Harris, MDiv

http://www.harrisministries.org

Article VII : Heaven's Regulations and *The Choice* for the Angels

Section III :

Heaven is a place of true worship, designed to be a home for God and his angels. The angels can come and go as they please. These free moral agents have access to every room, area and place in Heaven while completing their tasks for their divine assignment. The Creator in Heaven agrees to provide luxuries for such beings and make sure all of Heaven and all its operations are running smoothly.

In the unlikely event an angel wants to discontinue being functional in their task or start in with behavior contrary to his primary role, as a preliminary option, several steps will be taken. First, there will be a meeting with the angel to try to unite disorderly parties. This will take place at the Creator's discretion. A face to face confrontation will happen between God and Angel(s) to discuss the cause of this Angel's new development as well as come up with existing solutions for any issues that arise.

If no solution can be found, see Section IV, Note I

Section IV:

The keys to the Kingdom belong solely to the Creator of the Heavens. The keys to the Kingdom shall remain with God at all times. No angel shall have nor will be given the keys to the Kingdom unless first agreed upon by the Holy Trinity. Such instances are extreme and only to be decided as individual cases arise. An agreement between all God-parties will have one anonymous vote as to who is to receive the keys to the Kingdom besides the Almighty.

Note 1: If an angel is presently demonstrating action contrary to their anointed behavior and a solution is not found, the rule stands: there is no rebellion in Heaven. Safely monitor the being's present state and judge the condition of the being's heart towards Heaven and its Creator. If decided an action is deemed unlawful, the angel will suffer the consequence written in Note II.

If an angelic being also takes the keys to the Kingdom without being given the appropriate right from the Holy Trinity, the angel(s) will suffer the consequence written in Note II.

Note II: Any party who rebels to the above laws will face dire consequences. Any angel doomed to leave Heaven will be stripped from their title and position, never be allowed back in. A cursed option awaits them. These pre-mentioned parties will be cast out of Heaven after a honorable procession of five trumpets. After such procession, the rebellious parties will be driven out of Heaven. Forever.

God Almighty: _____
                        Signature

Jesus Christ: _____
                        Signature

Holy Spirit: _____
                        Signature

Chapter 1

I don't even know what to say. I have been in my office for hours. Days. The door is closed. Jesus and the Holy Spirit have been trying to encourage me and cheer me up.

Fortunately, they have been handling my affairs for me while I take this time off.

They keep saying we're prepared for this. That it's going to be okay.

They keep telling me we can rebuild and make all things new again.

The plan book lies face down on the hard, black desk, pages with the Spirit's handwriting inching out of it. He needs me to sign off on Heaven's Handbook for the Creation Project before we can go on to the next Project. I see the line where I need to sign my name.

If I sign that, it means it's over. It really is over.

Why didn't my friend just stay with me? I had prepared a different ending for him. It was supposed to lead to his promotion.

I am desperately holding on to Luce's Promotion Project. Why didn't he just take it? I had so much prepared for him. I had such high hopes. I had such great plans if he had just waited. If he had just trusted me...

The next Project is the Humanity Restoration Project. The papers are staring at me, unopened. I didn't want to reach this point. Not yet.

I look over at my panoramic display of the first blueprints of the Creation plan I created.

My keys are nestled safely in the solid gold lock. I used to have two sets of keys. Now I only have one.

I tried. I tried so hard to keep him.

And now my kids...my kids are going to be - - -

This was never my plan, but it's the risk I took. We made a project just for this occasion...it doesn't change the fact that my loved ones are gone...those who have been with me since the beginning. Gone. Gone in an instant. Just like that.

I pace back and forth, shaking my head.

I never wanted this. It didn't have to be this way!

I violently throw away Luce's Promotion Project.

Please leave me alone with my thoughts.

Maybe if I just go back to the beginning...I can process what *just* happened.

✶✶✶✶✶

"Hey, Barachiel! Keep setting up the wide arches! I need this to be a magnificent place!" I scream at the workers building my Kingdom. "You're doing a great job, Daniel!" I wave at a couple pulling together a load of crystals and diamonds. Another worker carrying light fixtures walks by me. There was a lot of activity going on in the center of the Plaza.

"Is this size for the front bridge okay?" Vehuel, one of the managers of this Heaven Expansion Project holds out a sheet for me to review. I flip through the notes and procedures. She stares at me, probably hoping I don't make any more changes.

This group has been so patient with me during this entire ordeal! Their work is incredible and much appreciated!

Though I made this land from scratch, I still wanted my angels to have assignments given by me personally, and those selected for construction help beautify my Kingdom. Each angel has a purpose and a reason for being created. I had to make them useful to keep the Kingdom going.

My angels in charge of construction were all wearing their white hard hats, but dressed in the finest, most comfortable white pants and shirt with a red embroidered 'GK' on the front with a pair of wings in the logo. It's easier for these particular workers to wear pants, but some in other departments wear robes, others suits, some white skirts; whatever fits their role and design. Every unique ensemble my angels wear is custom made by our finest tailor on staff. Every so often a new, clean outfit is delivered to each angel at the angel bay, a place designed specifically for my angels to stay.

It was indeed My Kingdom, **G**od's **K**ingdom and I have the **GK** logo everywhere to state my domain over this paradise. This is a place of pure joy, order, and productive work. There is no illness, doubt or fear, a world free from sickness, war, crime and anything harmful. Of course, absolutely no rebellion is tolerated!

The whole city is lighted by **my** glory, so it is lit all the time here in the Heavenly hub where one can worship and serve, fellowship and learn all with joy, contentment, and purpose.

"Good. Ruby walkways. Perfect. Gold streets. Good. Good. Where will the pearl gates go?" I ask Vehuel, her face radiating in goodness just as I made her.

"We were thinking over by the entrance of Heaven. We thought it would look nice as the first thing you see," she said, adjusting her hard hat.

"Yes. I approve! Only let's make 12 pearl gates; three on the north, three on the east, south, and west." I move as I point in the directions. "Thank you!" I sign at the bottom of the procedure sheet and let her get back to work. I have to sign off on everything that happens here. Normal protocol.

I am going to be so excited when all of this gets done! Of course, I have *unlimited* space so we can expand forever if we wanted. I laugh at this and enter into my office, walking through a wall of plastic covering.

I would invite you into the main Palace but it's currently being renovated.

I go into my makeshift office with plywood and plaster hanging down. Sawdust, papers, and notes are strewn all over my black desk. Boxes of notebooks are shoved in the corner.

I know it seems messy now, but once everything's done, it'll be beautiful!

The best laid out plans always take time.

I sit down and evaluate my agenda:

Preparing with Menu Meals with the Chef ✓

Precious Gem placement in Plaza ✓

Check in with Construction Crew ✓

4

What's next on the list? Ah, yes:

Meet with the worshippers.

I actually have plans to create a minute by minute time system so that my agenda can be more on a fixed time frame.

What is a minute you ask? I know. Everything is eternal here. I'll have to explain it later. It's hard to conceive the supernatural process translating into the natural. But stay with me. I'll show you *just that* for so many of my projects are in the works!

All these angels in Heaven meet with me regularly. They see my face and hear my voice. I need them to know that I am here for them, with them and that I support and love them. That's my job: to handle all the needs of Heaven and all the angels. It's a job I love and I take my role as friend, advisor and mentor very seriously!

I put my list of events away.

Let me share something with you. Something I've been working on. It's called the Creation Project.

I open my drawer and take out a few stencil drawings of the next project I have planned.

I'm going to expand. That's right, expand my Heavenly realm! Create more heavens! Create more life! The stencil drawings are something I came up with that I haven't shared with anyone *yet*, but the idea of it is yanking at my heartstrings!

Also, let me be the first to tell you what's next!

I stretch out all of my designs on the desk, moving the current clutter aside, rolling out the drawings of a male and a female.

I call them 'my Kids'; sharing **my** heartbeat, sharing **my** characteristics. This one to the left with the dark hair and brown eyes, he will be tall and masculine.

Near his sketch is a list of names written and crossed out: Isaiah ~~Jacob~~ ~~Daniel~~ Adam Alexander Vincent ~~Demetri~~

His name will be strong, anointed and will showcase his mature nature. I'm still in the development phase. I know any one of these names will work.

This other sketch here is the image of his female counterpart. I want there to be two of these humans (just to start). *She* will be full of beauty, femininity, and grace. She will be quite special to me! I feel like her name should be Abigail which means "Father's joy." And I know she will be **that** to me; it will be her higher purpose!

Both humans will stand on two legs with two arms like my angels. They will breathe from their nose and talk with their mouth also just like my angels. It's almost like I made Heaven first in preparation for this new development. I'm beyond excited, and nervous too. I instinctively fiddle with the one set of keys around my neck. The other set is safely in the gold safe. I look at this rough draft of a plan every chance I get. I cannot **wait** to continue on it. But for right now, there is still so much left here to do!

I put the designs back, folded and tucked neatly into the drawer.

"Knock! Knock!" Lucifer comes in smiling.

Oh good!

Let me introduce you to my very best friend in all of Heaven! I've created him special than the other angels. He has this incredibly massive wingspan with six wings! It's ridiculous! I feel like I went a little overboard when I made him! He is huge in size like the archangels and leads worship with the Seraphims.

I'll explain more about those group of angels later. I have a meeting with the worship team. You'll meet the Seraphims then.

Luce and I had a tight bond *right* from the beginning and have been inseparable ever since! He wears the same light fitting white uniform but with a red music note next to the GK logo.

I look at Luce. I remember when he was made. I remember when all my angels were made! But *he* was always special to me. The way he looks is so stunning: brilliant yellow eyes, his iced blonde hair, and his music - oh! His music! He's extraordinarily talented! He can put me in a better mood from just one note! I assigned him head of the Worship Department quickly and he has made some fantastic tunes for Heaven! He has been so close to me and I find his presence soothing and his friendship such a relief to have!

I put Luce in charge of about one-third of my kingdom. He *should* be very happy with the position of power I've given him, but it seems he always wants to be promoted from one higher position to the next. I constantly wonder...did I give him *too* much power? *Too* much ambition? I created him with such charisma, strength and might. It's hard to control, sometimes.

I actually have great plans for him! I want to give him the highest of all positions. No other angel has this position! He will report *directly* under me and will stay close to me in leadership and authority. It's a project I've been planning for a while...a surprise for him, really. It's called Luce's Promotion Project. I can't wait. I can't wait to see his expression! But that's not until later.

Luce plops himself on the leather chair in front of my cluttered desk and picks up my small plastic display of the new Palace being built. A big portrait of me smiling with the gold letters GK are scripted on the front.

"When am I going to have my own office?" he quickly asks. "I am sharing a desk with an archangel who grunts while he works."

"Hey! Leave Gabe out of this!" I respond, taking the display from Luce realizing then that I'm basically holding the future of Heaven in my hands.

"Your workspace will be done soon enough," I laugh.

"Want to take a little break? Walk for a bit?" My friend suggested.

"But I have all this work to do. And the boss needs to set an example..."

♪♫♬ "Rest in Heaven's care. Know that you lead magnificent. Trust in your design. And know how much your angels love you." ♪♫♬ Lucifer starts to sing.

"Okay. Okay," I smile. "Just for a little bit." I go to the gold safe near the corner of the room and turn the dial to open the door using my favorite number: 7-7-7. I pick up the remaining set of keys to the Kingdom and place it around my neck, the shining gold glittering to the touch embroidered with GK on them. I can't go anywhere without these two sets of keys.

We walk outside to the noise of busyness, construction and heavy machinery from the crew working and shouting to each other. We walk and talk past the cafeteria which will soon be the Main Dining Hall and past the orchestra room which will soon be the Worship Center.

So many plans in the making!

This city is filled with a brilliance of costly stones and crystal clear jasper. The outer walls are made of precious jewels. The sapphire gems, turquoise blue, and amethyst stones glitter back at me majestically.

As we walk, I notice the gently placed signs that read: "This is a peaceful environment. There is no rebellion in Heaven. You have a *choice. Choose* **Love**."

It was the Spirit's idea to post those signs. He would love it if we could continue through all of our current and future projects without any distractions. I would like that too.

We are always reminding our angels why they are made and what they're divine purpose is.

I would hate for any of them to forget...

We walk to one of the central areas of Heaven, a sort of oasis: a massive garden of every flower, shrub, and tree creating the finest fruit: apples, pears, blueberries, and oranges. The place I make next, I want to expand on this garden. I call this area my Garden of Solace. I breathe in the fresh air and smile at the beauty of this pristine nature. The main tree, a rich magnificence of perfection I specifically call the Tree of Life, has a waterfall cascading down which foams at the bottom and forms a river that flows through the entire city of Heaven. Such beauty!

Lining that river are trees that bear mouthwatering fruit. I see angels resting under trees, taking fruit and eating as they continue their walk. I see some angels playing near the river.

Every soft plant turns to me as I sit on the emerald bench, knowing that its growth depends on nothing but me, my power and my love. I reach down to hold a rose gently in my palm, its petals embracing my touch. My friend sits on the nearby glass rock carved as a seat.

"What's on your mind?" Lucifer asks as I get lost in the contradiction of it all; one area of my mind is always looking ahead and one area seems in the moment.

"Nothing," I sigh.

"You can tell me." Lucifer plucks a delicate rose and starts pulling at it, each crimson petal plummeting to the ground.

I watch him and don't stop his mistreatment. His actions are his own.

"I just want to make sure that what I am doing is beneficial for everyone," I respond.

"I think so," Luce replied. "I mean, plenty of enough room for all of your angels."

"I wasn't just talking about the angels," I said.

"No? What then?"

I shake my head a little, unsure of whether I should reveal anything at this time. But Luce was looking at me with such sincerity and understanding. I know I can trust him.

"I'm going to expand."

"<u>More?</u> What are you? A God who wants it **all**?" He then pretends to mock me with a harmless impression: "I AM GOD. HEAR ME ROAR!"

I laugh.

"Oh!?" Suddenly his expression lights up. "Are you going to assign managers for this new expansion?" He asks. "Because if so, can I volunteer?" He raises his hand in a joking-like manner. "I would **love** to have some more authority around here."

"I'm still at the beginning stages," I answer. "Plus, you <u>do</u> have authority."

"Not enough..." I hear him mumble.

"What did you say?"

"Nothing. Just...keep me informed. I can always help, you know that."

"I know. I was going to talk about the details of this upcoming project at the Feast and Fellowship."

I look back out at the on-going construction happening around me, the sight of angels working with such diligence; painting, molding, welding.

I felt a tenseness. A shiver crawled through me. I looked at my friend. "Just stay with me, Luce. No matter what happens, just stay with me" I say with a little more seriousness than I intended.

"Of course. Where else would I go?" He almost looked confused.

I was about to say something but I hear someone clear their throat. I look up.

The Holy Spirit walks up with a clipboard and some notes. "Sorry to interrupt."

The Spirit looks *just like* me. He has the same joy for life, amazing creativity, the same eye for detail and the same organized demeanor (way more organized than me!). The Holy Spirit is a spirit, a divine replica of me, translucent in his being. We call him 'The Spirit'. It's pretty casual here in Heaven.

"You know, Lucifer," the Spirit chimed in. "We could use some of your musical talent to create more masterpieces to teach the choir."

"I've already done that," Luce was quick to respond.

"You can implement plans on how to create better communication tactics for the throne room meetings. You have a hand in protecting God's holiness, do you not? I would love for you to use your extra time learning about the throne room developments. We could certainly use you further in this."

"I can work on that..." Luce retorted slowly.

The Spirit kept looking at him.

"Okay. I can work on that *now*," Luce said, getting up. "I guess I have some work to get back to. Can't wait to sit next to that grunting brute again!" He grunts in sport as he walks away.

I wave goodbye to him and talk with the Holy Spirit a bit, getting up off the bench.

"You always assign Luce more work whenever you see him. As if you are almost babysitting him," I have to comment to the Spirit as soon as my friend is out of earshot.

"I am just trying to make sure he feels useful here. I don't ever want him to forget his purpose."

I look down. "I know what you are trying to do."

"Are you still preparing for his Promotion Project to happen?" The Spirit asks inquisitively.

"It's either that...or..." I respond with sad eyes.

"Let's not talk about any of this just yet," the Spirit changes the subject. "I just finished the revisions in the Heaven

Handbook. Section Three is complete as you requested. I was hoping you could look them over. You can sign here," he points.

He gives me the pages from the Handbook with the new rules.

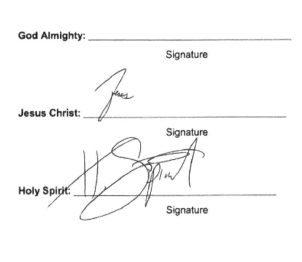

God Almighty: _____
                              Signature

Jesus Christ: _____
                              Signature

Holy Spirit: _____
                              Signature

It's the new regulations to Heaven. I felt like the previous rules had to be regulated a bit and the consequences had to be instituted just a little more.

I skim over its contents. Basically, free moral agents have access to every room, area, and place in Heaven when completing their tasks for their divine assignment. The Creator in Heaven (me) agrees to provide luxuries for such beings and makes sure all of Heaven is content and all operations are running smoothly. In the unlikely event an angel wants to discontinue being functional in their task or starts in with behavior contrary to his primary role, as a preliminary option, several steps will be taken. First, there will be a meeting with the angel to try to unite disorderly parties.

Yada... yada... yada.

The keys to the Kingdom belong solely to the Creator of the Heavens. The keys to the Kingdom shall remain with God at all times. No angel shall have or will be given the keys to the Kingdom.

Reading on...

Any angel doomed to leave Heaven will be stripped from their title and position, never to be allowed back in. Any party who rebels to these laws will face dire consequences. A cursed option awaits them. These pre-mentioned parties will be cast out of Heaven after an honorable procession of five trumpets.

"You know me. I always have a Plan B," The Spirit's answer for everything as I reluctantly sign on the bottom line.

Let's hope it never comes to this!

I designed my angels to stay with me for all eternity. Their home is here.

"Do you want to go over the Humanity Restoration Project now or later?" The Spirit asks while putting the signed forms in a designated folder.

I close my eyes at the thought of this Project. "Is that the one where one of us lives on Earth?"

"Yes. I just need you to approve on a few details."

"Later," I answer quickly. "The *choice* hasn't been made yet."

"Of course. Well, your appointment with the worshippers is right now," He said. "They are waiting for you."

We walk up to the orchestra room and I go inside to greet my Heavenly music makers.

Yes, it is *that* time for my choir of angels to sing to me, even with the loud construction noise in the back. They always request me as their audience and it is an honor to sit in the front row!

This worship team is made up of a specific kind of angel: *Seraphims* who are the highest order of choir angels. *Any* angel can sing to me but these were *made* specifically for worship! Each Seraphim has six wings (like Luce but less of a wingspan): two with the ability to cover their faces, two covering their feet, and two for flying. They sometimes keep their wingspan around their sides as to not bump into the other angel next to them while they all sing together in unison.

The orchestra room has a stage, an auditorium, a backstage for performers and of course plush red velvet seats for the audience. Right now it is a great place for concerts, speeches, meetings and the like. All the angels seat comfortably, leaving no room for anyone extra. This will be expanded too, which is to explain the loud sound of hammers, drilling, and chainsaws echoing down the hallways.

There is a huge picture of Luce in the orchestra room in the back. He put it up there on his own. He is posing with his GK white robe while holding up his hand as if he's conducting the orchestra.

I let him keep it up. No harm in that, since he <u>does</u> lead worship here every day.

I wonder about him though. I often think about his *choice*. I want him to stay with me.

I shift my attention to the front as I look at Jehoel, Seraphiel, Metatron, Hashmal, Jequn, and all the others on stage, performing their hearts out for me. Such passion! Jequn takes the microphone and sings alongside Hashmal. Others are backup singers on the side. They just explode their devotion for me and they sing about their love of being here in Heaven with me.

So precious! I feel so loved!

I smile so wide and clap to the music!

♪♫♬ *"Holy! Holy! Holy is the Lord of Hosts! Sing to the One who created it all! Sing to the One in charge of Heaven! Praise to the God of all angels and Master of all design!"* ♪♫♬

Their voices are triumphant in volume and melody. Though they sing in harmony, I promise I could hear **all** of Heaven singing with them, the swaying of the rich trees, the golden rocks on the streets moving to the tune, the archangels working together in unison to the song. I absolutely love being sung to, it truly encourages my spirit!

I can do this.

We <u>will</u> continue with these upcoming projects.

The encouragement of these beings empower me!

I <u>can</u> complete the plans I have made and perhaps give the angels more friends to sing with!

Perhaps.

Chapter 2

"**A**nd we give thanks for all we have. Amen." The Spirit finished his prayer for all the awaiting angels. I'm standing right beside him.

The Spirit continues, "Now remember our new regulations and consider the signs. Stay away from what's not yours." I hold up my keys as a demonstration. "Always *choose* love. We don't want any rebellion here. This place is for you. Let's keep it beautiful. We love you all."

I scream "Let's eat!" and clap my hands loudly.

The Spirit leads the prayer and says the same speech right before the start of Feast and Fellowship which takes place in the cafeteria, a place near the Plaza where all the angels can stop their tasks, sit and dine together.

This area opens up to one large room with a space in the back for the cooks and crew. There are multiple round ivory tables set up around the space with matching chairs. The food is self-serve and in the middle of the room are trays keeping the food warm. The drink and dessert tables stay off to the side.

Though none of us here *need* food to eat, it's an amazing time for all of Heaven to sit in front of a banquet prepared by the finest chefs.

These divine dishes range from a silky dark canopy of chocolate desserts, a wide range of moist vegetables steaming from the plates, cheese, bread and every kind of fresh fruit picked right here from the Garden of Solace placed in the most stunning display!

I have created these meals to serve all of Heaven. In the near future, I plan on taking these ideas to a **new** place and I will make sure that the same fruits and vegetables will be grown and harvested, the same extravagant foods will be savored! I want to bring **all** the delicacies of Heaven into this new project. I truly cannot wait!

I sit next to my closest confidantes at the table by the front. It's a packed place so the sounds of overheard conversations, plates hitting tables and angels moving through the single file line for a plated meal are all I hear as the head Chef places my meal in front of me.

The Godhead gets the meals prepared personally.

I see everyone in Heaven right here and during this outing, it's a way for me to be available to every angel. All my angels gather together in this one room and each ranked as I made them.

The Seraphims from earlier are together, their wings going every which way as they continue through the food line, one angel trying not to get a wing in the chocolate pudding!

The Cherubims are double-winged and have such a wide wingspan. They sometimes wait to get their food last as to not hit anyone in the face!

Of course, the conversations dim when the Archangels walk in, Michael leading the way with Gabriel, Raphiel and Cassiel along with the rest in their large group. Grandeur in their stature and confidence, they make their way to their respective table.

All my angels are strong and intelligent in their function and order, though some have wings and others don't, some are huge in size and some are smaller. It never matters to me. Each one is perfect the way that I created them!

"Hey, Agla and Kailon!" I yell at my favorite pair. These two are inseparable! They do everything together. Agla teaches management training in one of the conference rooms and Kailon is under Luce in the Worship Choir. They wave back and of course, they find a place to sit next to each other.

The seat on my right belongs to Jesus Christ and you've already met the Holy Spirit who sits on my left, the only two who are allowed to sit at the front table with me. We three face the massive room of angels sitting with their friends, a mesh of white and wings. The Spirit is always so busy, readily planning his next move to make sure everything I say goes absolutely, accurately right. It's no surprise, he brought his work to the table to look over.

Jesus, on the other hand ...where is he? I look across the room. Oh! I see him! He's over by the food trays! He's so friendly towards everyone! He looks *just like* me but shorter and a bit younger. He hasn't eaten a bite out of his meal yet for he likes to serve the angels their food, shake their hands, giving them high-five's and hugs, and listening to their stories. I smile watching him work. His love is so contagious!

I take off my keys and place them on the table right in front of me as Luce jumps right into Jesus' empty chair and helps himself to Jesus' meal, scarfing up the vegetable plate in two bites, leaving just some food and the thin unleavened bread only Jesus loves to eat.

"Hungry?" I ask, laughing.

"When I get my keys, mine will say LK," Luce suggested, eyeing my keys on the table.

"Well, Luce, it's not your kingdom," I remind him.

"Yea. I know...I was just joking! So, what's the plan you were going to talk about over the meal?" Lucifer asks instantly, his yellow eyes staring into mine, his feathers drawing back in anticipation. He grabs at my keys and plays with them for a bit.

"Oh. I wasn't going to share that publicly just yet. I was going to talk to this closed group right here." I pointed to the Holy Spirit who was putting away his notes.

"You can tell me, though. I mean, we're best friends. And plus, look. Jesus isn't even - -"

"I'm here now!" Jesus said, his face a little flushed with a huge smile on his face. "Lucifer!!" Jesus places his hands on Luce's shoulders. "Good to see you! Love the new song you sang! ♪♫♬ *Praise all of Heaven and rejoice! The Lord is good to all of us. Rejoice!*♪♫♬" Jesus sings loudly and a little off key.

Lucifer gets up off the chair, not without grabbing Jesus' glass of red wine, drinking right from it. "Thanks. Happy you like it."

"Luce," I ask, reaching my hand out. "Aren't you forgetting something?"

"Oh. Yeah. Sorry." He then places my keys in my hand, almost reluctantly.

"I'll talk to you tomorrow," I say to Luce as he walks off. "For now, just have fun with your friends. I'm sure they would love to see you."

"So, you have my undivided attention," says the Spirit. Jesus is eating while looking at me, finally getting to his half-eaten meal while everyone else in the room is going back up for seconds.

"I think it's time," I say with excitement. "I think we need to initiate the Creation Project."

Jesus stopped eating and looked at me seriously. "Are you sure? You know what that means?"

"I do."

The Holy Spirit looked just as concerned. "If we get started on this now...that means..."

I finish his sentence. "...that means *choices* will be made. Yes, I know. I have to believe the right *choice* will be made."

Jesus and the Spirit take a long look at each other.

"Guys," I assure them. "Nothing's happened yet. And I can't stop progress. And I want to meet them!!! I want to show off my glory! My power!"

"We are just afraid that - -" Jesus started to say.

I stopped him immediately. "Since when has **fear** ever stopped us? If we wanted safety, it would have been just us three for eternity."

Jesus nods. "You're right."

"Is this *just* about creating your humans?" The Spirit inquired.

"No," I answer. "This is **all** for my humans! Surely you must know this! Surely you must know how much I love them!"

Jesus smiles. "And you haven't even made them yet!" Jesus stopped and was now digging into the rich dessert the baker had just brought out.

The Holy Spirit took out his notebook to scribble something as we talked as if taking notes. He then tapped his pen on the table, deep in thought as if playing out various scenarios in his head. "Well," the Spirit then added. "We do have a Plan B."

"See!!" I announce to even myself. "We have a Plan B!"

Jesus finally spoke up, putting his food down. "I just don't want you to get your heart broken."

I nod but felt the need to remind him, "Remember what we agreed on when we formed Heaven and the angels? We *could* get rejected but we love them anyway. Because **love** always wins."

"I'm excited to meet my friends. I know they'll be friends for life," Jesus cried out!

I then take out the designs of humanity from my pocket, gently unfold them and place them towards my confidantes.

I look down at the designs with such love. "Let me make them!"

"I am not stopping you," the Spirit calmly stated. "I just want you to remember that this is unpredictable. You don't know how they are going to behave." He then picks up one of my drawings and examines it as if considering the intense possibilities.

"Look," I say, remaining positive. "My angels have free will. *They* can leave anytime and no one has. They love it here and I love them! And with these new beings, I will love them too! I want to be the most important part of their lives!"

"I know you do…" the Spirit trailed off. "Just remember, you don't *have* to do this."

"No," I agree. "But I really really want to!"

The Spirit flipped through the pages of his notebook to write more ideas. "There's something to consider before the project begins. Do you want to send one of our own angels to watch over your humans and personally guard them?" the Holy Spirit asked. "I know Luce has been begging for a promotion."

I thought for a moment. "As of right now, I want these new creatures to rely on me **personally**. I want them to come to me if they need anything. I want to be their dad in so many ways!"

"I love it! Can I be their big brother?" Jesus nodded. I think he was energetic from all the food he just gulped down.

"Well, I am always behind you in anything you do," the Spirit said, closing his binder of notes. "Where should we start and when?"

"Very soon. I want to officially announce all of this to the family first," I say as I see most of my angels leaving the cafeteria with big smiles on their faces. They wave in our direction as we wave back.

The cafeteria workers are now coming out to collect the remaining food on the tables. I am hoping they'll like the news of this <u>new</u> family.

Let's hope.

Chapter 3

I review my plan book over and over again. The new diagram showcasing displays of brilliant color and design is behind me presenting the humans, nature and animals all in one massive diorama. This was all made for the official great "reveal" of the plans.

I think about what it's going to take to get all this completed, all the time I'm going to have to devote to this Creation project. I replay the same question in my head. Will this work like I want it to work? I can't leave anything out! I need the right ingredients. The temperature has to be just so. The intricacies of my creation have to be able to function properly. I have to arrange soil, nutrients and oxygen which I'm all making from scratch. I have to create human organs that are ongoing in their efforts to preserve life. Is this an insane idea? Am I not satisfied with what I have in Heaven? My angels love me. I have friends here. I look down at the keys around my neck. What exactly am I wanting?

I was in my office, alone.

I can do so much thinking alone, away from the crowds.

Then, I saw it. I saw the future playing out in front of me. It was as if this moment was happening right here, right now. "Daddy?" One of my kids looks for me, "Can you play with me? I want you with me!" I see one little girl smiling and laughing, playing in the Garden I've made for her. "Come join us! Walk with us!" She waves at me! I see a whole generation of my creation enjoying what I have made for them, perfectly content with themselves. Even the animals all seem incredibly happy. A ferocious-looking animal rests gently next to a white, fluffy animal who doesn't even flinch when the predator approaches. It was quiet, calm and peaceful. This creation depends on me, they trust me, and they open another side of my heart. This unique relationship is one I desperately long for! I don't want a worker, not a planner, not an organizer, not a busybody, but a **true** friend, one who wants just **me**, one I can love *forever*.

The noise of a chainsaw woke me up out of this instant daydream, the vision dissolving in front of me. I blink and I am staring at my messy office, the Humanity Restoration Project and Luce's Promotion Project on my black desk staring back at me.

The Humanity Restoration Project: a project I never intended on using. I close my eyes and breathe deep.

"A *choice* has not been made yet," I say, my eyes still closed.

Love <u>always</u> wins. I know this! I invented it that way!

I breathe in, nodding my head and opening my eyes.

For now, I *must* go on with my plans, for the sake of my kids! For their lives. For their future. For the possibilities of something more...

I situate my papers and fold up the drawing boards and sketches. I sure have a lot to talk about with my fellow angels. I hope they approve of this new expansion.

*****

"Hello everyone!" I walk into a packed auditorium in the orchestra room. In front of me is a sea of my angels sitting down, talking among themselves, and some walking around trying to find a seat. Some of the larger archangels are standing in the back. Jesus and the Holy Spirit stand at the pulpit on the front of the stage, waiting for me to enter. I see my friend, Luce, in the front row. Even with all this support, I still feel nervous to start this process...knowing what I know.

I get to the microphone with the front stage lights beaming on me.

"Thank you all for coming. I have a big announcement. You are probably wondering why I am calling a Heaven-wide meeting. Well, I am going to introduce you to some things I have been working on and then I can answer questions when I'm done."

Jesus and the Spirit open the wide panoramic display showcasing what has been on my mind for a long time: the white stars, the massive planets, the outrageous wildlife, and my special beings all staring back.

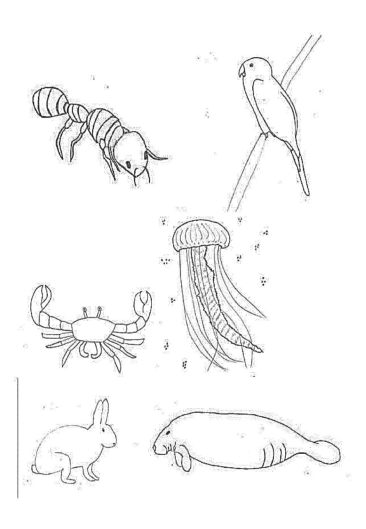

"So, as you can see, I am going to *expand* Heaven. I know what you are thinking. We just launched the Heaven Expansion Project a short while ago. Why am I taking on another? Well, I want the current workers to continue building the Palace up to speed and I want the jewelers to keep up their amazing job of creating beauty within Heaven. *This* project I am taking on through **my** own efforts. It will not be created or worked on by any angel in this place. Only **I** will create this masterpiece you see behind me. I was inspired one day at my Garden of Solace:

the trees, the greenery, the waterfall! I want this new creation to be plentiful, a tapestry of wonderful plants and animals. I want to create multiple planets, many terrains and temperatures, vast oceans and topography! But I want this <u>one</u> planet to host my humans. It will involve life, precise movement, exquisite timing, and divine accuracy! And my pride and joy I want to introduce you to is *this*, right here. A new community of beings!"

Jesus then moves my big designs of human beings to the front of the stage showing the boy's face and sketches of what he will look like. And finally, Abigail, her long flowing hair and similar yet different sketches from her male counterpart.

"They will walk on two legs," I continue. "I will instill a destiny on their life and they will live for me, because of me *and* with me. They will get their nutrients from the Earth that I will provide for them. This will be a new sort of Creation. I will call them by a personal name that I will come up with myself. They will be similar to me in so many ways! They will act like me. And they will have my love, my life and my joy. The Spirit will give each human a brain, a unique personality and a different approach to life. This is going to be an amazing development and I wanted to keep all of you fully informed."

I close my eyes for a brief second and breathe in and out slowly.

I did it! I'm finally sharing my heart and vision with my Heavenly family. The first step has begun.

"Okay," said the Spirit, coming up to the mic. "We can answer a few questions at this time."

Many hands were raised as I saw angels talking and whispering among themselves. Some had shocked expressions on their faces like they didn't know what to think. Others smiled and applauded. It was definitely a mixed room.

"Yes. In the back. Archangel Michael. You have a question," the Holy Spirit monitored the audience with such diligence.

Archangel Michael comes forward from the back.

"I am behind you one hundred percent, God," Michael commented with such force "If you want me to be a defender to your new Earth, I will do so. My team and I will serve to guard your new creatures!"

I waved my hand at the suggestion. "Thank you and my entire team of Archangels! At this time, your help will not be necessary. Not on this current Project. I plan to walk among my humans continually. My purpose for them is to live joyously and eternally."

Another hand was raised. "Won't you be sacrificing time away from your angels and away from Heaven?" Another angel, Amriel wanted to know.

"That's just it!" I answer. "I want this to be an open forum, a place where all of you angels can come and go as you please. I mean, look around! I made *this* and I think it's going quite well. You all are happy!"

"A question. Zophiel." The Holy Spirit was moving on quickly around the room.

"Yes," Zophiel said, getting up from one of the middle seats. "We do have assignments here! Will we be given *more* work?"

I thought for a moment before continuing. " I **am** thinking on a future basis of assigning angels down to Earth to check in with these mortals every so often just to serve them and assist them - - -"

"Serve *them*?" someone from the audience screamed. "They should be serving *us*!"

"Yeah! You make a new set of creatures and now <u>we</u> are supposed to be used at their every beckon call?" Another demanded.

"Don't you forget who *we* are?" shouted another. The auditorium became an uproar of voices.

"Wow..." I whisper and shake my head. Jesus looks over at me, concerned.

"Silence! All of you!" Lucifer stands up from the front row. The *Morning Star* has gotten the attention of the room, his wings lifted at attention. Silence falls on the crowd. "This is God speaking. He knows best! **None** of us would be here without him! He provided this great place for us to live and eat and do our bidding. So he's asking us for a favor! *Surely*, we can respect his wishes! *Surely*, we can serve under his leadership!" Lucifer's little speech continued to amaze and awe the audience as he got up and walked around the room. "Those who are against this idea, come see me! I will assure you as to why this plan needs to continue!"

I walked toward Jesus. "I have to leave."

"Are you okay?" he whispered.

"Yeah." My heart was completely hurt and confused. I appreciated Luce for jumping in, but I thought my plan would be a little more well-received and instead, I thought I was losing my audience...losing my angels...losing my family.

I fiddle with my keys at the thought.

"It's okay," Jesus comforted me. "We know the plans well. We can take it from here. You can go."

I smile and head out. Out past the grandeur of heaven. Out. Out. Far. Far. Away.

To my reserved spot where I can climb up and sit peacefully, where I can go and clear my mind. This holy mountain is located on the back side of the city, a grandeur rock designed to overlook all of Heaven. Instead, I face the other way. I look out into the black nothingness; the corner of where Heaven ends. It's where I can sit and think.

I welcome the quietness and breathe in the stillness.

I knew Jesus and the Holy Spirit would be okay without me. They see the plans clearly and they can answer any more questions.

I breathe in and out.

This is the hard part. Letting go of the familiar. Stepping out into the unknown. Trading stability for controlled chaos. Where the future meets the present.

I close my eyes.

I have to continue, even with this uproar. Because I know even **my** plans seem disorderly in the beginning. My angels need to have a little faith in me....

"Knock! Knock!"

I quickly open my eyes.

"Are you hiding?" I look up to see those powerful yellow eyes staring at me.

Lucifer came up, his massive wingspan down by his side. He sat right next to me. I knew *he* would know where I was.

"That was quite a performance you put on," Luce laughed. I instantly felt relieved to see him.

"Thanks for what you did back there. I didn't want any of my angels to be upset. It was like they didn't trust me," I sighed.

"No. That's wasn't it." Lucifer looked in front of him, the blackness staring right back at him. "I think they just don't want to share your love. They're afraid they might lose you."

I nodded, letting that truth sink in. "I didn't even get to explain that we would all be a family. That we would all be on the same side. Angels and humans will live in a perfect balance together."

"The Holy Spirit explained it. Don't worry." Luce put his hand on my shoulder for a second. "All the angels left content and happy. It was only just a few of the angels that seemed to shout at first with concern, but they all seemed okay afterward."

We were silent for a moment before my friend had to ask, "Are you *sure* you know what you are doing? I mean, why change things?"

I look at Luce and grab his arm. "Here. See what I am seeing!" Instantly the black sky in front of us became a red projector of things to come. Lucifer was stunned and marveled. The intricacies of the night sky. "So many stars!" He screamed. The complexities of the planets, the marvelous sight of the solar systems. Lucifer was joyful at the noises the animals would make, the vastness of the ocean. Now, the scene unfolded to the human life: the beating pulse of the human heart, the mystery of the human brain, the plans of childbirth, and the organs inside the human body working and functioning together.

He reaches out his hands to grab at one of the smiling women right as the screen vanished and all that was left was a blanket of silence and darkness.

"Oh, my," Lucifer sat, stunned. "I - - - I had no idea it would be *that* wonderful!"

I looked at him. "Oh. It will be."

When I looked, he seemed to have a curious expression on his face.

"What is it?" I ask.

"Will the humans be able to make decisions like us?"

"Of course! I gave all my angels a *choice:* a *choice* to work, to eat, to rest and to *choose* me. I will provide that for my humans, too. I want them to love me. I *hope* they all love me."

Luce looked like he was deep in thought. I created this being next to me to hold infinite wisdom and superiority, to help me in my endeavors. I truly trust his insight.

"I don't think you should give your people free will," Luce finally said which surprised me.

"What? Why not?"

"I mean, you are forming them, right? You want to create a species who loves you. If you just instill a powerful force that draws them to *you* and to nothing else, they will always love you and you will never get your heart broken."

"My initial plan for this Creation..." I pause for a second before continuing. "Is for nothing bad to happen to them. Is something or someone bad going to come near them, Luce?"

Luce stopped, almost frowning like he sees something but doesn't know what. He shakes it off. "Giving them a *choice* might be their downfall. That's all I'm saying."

It was quiet before he finally looks at me. "It's a dangerous game. **True Love**. To give someone the *choice* to turn from you. That means they can *choose* to be away from you. Forever."

"You're absolutely right," I say firmly. "But how will I know if their love is real and genuine if I don't give them that *choice*? I see your concern, friend. But this decision I will not sway from. It's a risk I'm *just* going to have to take."

Chapter 4

"So I calmed everyone down," Jesus said. The Holy Spirit was pacing back and forth as if he was going through every detail in his head.

We were in my office; I was sitting on a small sofa near the window looking at the magnificence of Heaven being built. Construction workers walked past the window with a large ladder and a huge bucket of diamonds.

"Are you *sure* you want to continue? I mean, why now?" The Holy Spirit finally spoke up. "We can start this anytime. Maybe after the Heaven Expansion Project...I just don't want to see you getting your heart broken. You know the risk!"

"We **all** knew the risks! We wouldn't be <u>sitting</u> here in Heaven if we hadn't made a risk! I am going to *love* my creation." I say, turning to face the more sensible and reasonable side of my being.

"Yes," said Jesus, who was sitting at my desk looking through the papers of the Creation Project. "But will *they* love you?"

"They're going to! I just know it!" I scream, fully assured, standing up and facing my team. "I am going to provide <u>everything</u> for my humans! Water. Food. Relationships. Friendships. They can call on me whenever they want! I will be their healer, their provider, their friend and their God. I will be available to them for whatever they want and need! This is literally <u>all</u> for them!"

"You really *do* love them, don't you?" Jesus recognized this immediately, holding up the sketches I've made. Abigail's smile in the picture lit up the room. "And you haven't even met them, yet."

"No. Not yet. But when we officially do meet, I know it'll be a family homecoming!"

The office door flies open with the Archangel Gabriel announcing the big news. "We are all ready for you." All my archangels are so tall in stature and so serious about their work.

I sigh. "This is it. No turning back now," I say, making sure my keys are around my neck.

I look at the two other sides of the Trinity and nod to them as we leave my office, making our way to the center of the Plaza.

I see every single angel in Heaven lined up facing us, giving us room to walk through. The looks on their faces range from high expectation and joy to uncertainty and indifference, some needing evidence that what I'm saying is, in fact, a good thing.

Some angels slap me on the back or shake my hand as I walk through the crowd. Others are clapping as I walk by, noticing Kailon and Agla also applauding us. I know all these angels by name: "Thanks Eremiel. Thank you, Grigori! I appreciate your support, Nanael."

The Holy Spirit clutches the plan book tightly as we walk. Luce is waiting for me at the center, making sure to say "Good luck" along with a strong pat on the back. I knew he would be there for me!

Jesus looks a bit concerned but a sense of eagerness crawls on his face.

This is it.

"My friends. My angels!" I scream as we stop to face the crowd. "We will start the Creation Project! This will be a radiant start to our Kingdom and for our kind! A new family will emerge! Let this New Earth be your playground. I don't want any violence, war or negativity. Only peace, only love and only our family in Heaven to grow with this new Family. You will be a witness to the greatest creation ever conceived. Together, we will rule over it all."

The crowd of angels cheered, a massive sea of white wings and feathers!

I smiled.

I got their attention. Now, I have to deliver on my promise.

"Write this down. Day One," I scream.

Instantly, I vanish from my Heaven. All I see around me is the great abyss, a formless and empty space; the darkness I continually gaze at from my holy mountain now surrounds me on all sides. I would always look at this black - nothingness and the void would always stare right back at me with a sneering strength. But not today. Today, I can turn this nothing into something amazing.

Jesus was on my right-hand side and the Holy Spirit on my left. All around us was the darkness though my glory gave us ample light to see. But we needed more.

"Now," I said excitedly. "I need to make the planet they will live on. That's first."

I need a sphere, a perfect place in the center of this massive amount of infinite space.

"Why don't you just extend Heaven?" Holy Spirit suggested.

"No. I want to show off my glory. This is all brand new," I proudly announce.

I stretch out both hands and then place them together, zapping into existence power: waves of energy, combining and crashing, colliding and sparking, rolling violently as it matured together, forming gravitational and magnetic forces.

I watched this all unfold before me.

The liquid metal formed and hardened to form the core of this new planet, circulating currents as it meshed into one metal.

Working with this extreme power was so unpredictable, as I placed moveable elements into one area and as I stretched life into the cosmos.

"We need to use what **we** have to create more," Jesus suggested. "You wrote here you wanted Earth to resemble Heaven. Let's use parts of Heaven as an existing evidence of our footprints here..."

From where I was, I could get an ariel view of my Kingdom. I saw my massive Garden with the magnificent waterfall and the enormous Tree of Life in the middle.

"Yes," I agree. "Let's take the holy water from Heaven's waterfall and use it to create a living stream Earth will live on. It will nourish all life on the planet."

"Do we use ours? Do we borrow it?" The Holy Spirit asked.

"No. We use just some of it." I point to the water flowing and bubbling and churning down the massive tree.

"I got this," Jesus said. "Just call me *the Living Water*." He smiled. He then held out his hand as if controlling the elements. The water from the top of the Tree moved as if on command, flowing towards Jesus a thin line of water connecting from the top of the mountain stream.

"No. I don't want all of it," Jesus commanded.

The water stream then stopped in front of Jesus, the rest continued pouring down the edge of the waterfall and splashing down to the rocks on the bottom of the Tree.

But there was a horizontal stream of water facing Jesus and it just stood there, still moving rapidly as if pulsating with life. It was such a bizarre sight!

"Do you have it?" I ask.

"Yep. I got it." Jesus still had his hand out, the water obeying in one fine line.

"And where do we put that water?" The Holy Spirit asked, quickly reading through the pages of the game plan.

"We're putting in on the Earth. That water is detrimental to this place that will hold my new creation," I say with excitement.

"Okay, Holy Spirit. I need your help," Jesus said, still eyeing the moving water in front of him.

The Holy Spirit closed the book. "Yep, what do you need?"

"You have to make a sphere, a plane, a resting place for this water."

"Alright," the Holy Spirit thought for a moment. He then formed an area similar to the way He formed Heaven *all* that time ago, around the hot liquid metal in front of us, using that as a core for this new Earth.

I watched him work; the dedication in his eyes, the focus, the hope for the great possibilities of this Earth and its people.

It was a rather large area, a vast canvas, a huge amount of space that I could fill with all my imagination and wonder.

"What do you think?" the Spirit turned to me. "I mean, it's not finished yet, but it gives you an idea of how you might want to grow this area."

I look intently at the start of all this. It's a very plain, round sphere in front of me. Nothing added. Just an empty space. "It's perfect. For now, Jesus, go ahead and keep the water at the bottom of this new place. I'm going to look over my plans later and adjust all of this accordingly for Day 2."

I'm beginning to realize what's on paper doesn't necessarily translate when creating this new reality. I definitely have work cut out for me.

Jesus then placed the rushing water gently down on the new Earth. It did nothing but rush back and forth, aggressive waves being created as it bounced off of the walls, sides, and borders of the new space, almost as if excited to be used by the Lord of the Universe.

What stood in front of me was a sphere just hanging on nothing, a formless planet Earth suspended in the darkness. The liquid water from the hot surface of the core poured out a little. The Spirit hovered over this, blowing oxygen onto the water, cooling it down, his face reflecting as he passes.

At this point, my creation was just a ball of water. But I have more to add!

"This sphere will move so that this planet will be an ever-present revolving cycle of life and seasons, but the speed of its rotation has to be....just...so," I say as I put my hand on the top like a toy and turn it to what I felt was the right movement. "And I need to tilt it, like so. Exactly 23.5 degrees."

"It's funny," Jesus spoke up. "I didn't feel the tilt when I was living on the planet with your kids."

"No. You won't feel it. I made it that way," I commented.

"Wait!" the Spirit cut us off. "Are you talking about the Humanity Restoration Project?"

"Of course," Jesus smiles at the thought.

"Listen," the Spirit looks at you directly. Yes, you. The person reading this. "For the sake of our reader, let's stay in the present. Our kid will get confused if we explain how we are in the future *and* in the present."

"Sorry," Jesus says. He appears to where you are reading this. Right where you are. That's right, he sees you right now. "I'm just happy you are reading this story. It took a lot for **you** to get here..."

The Holy Spirit now appears to where you are.

"You are going to freak them out if they knew you were in the room!" The Spirit says.

"There used to be a time when they would embrace me!"

"So, not to brag, but I did a great job on this kid's eyes!" The Spirit watches you read.

"I know," Jesus smiles. "They sparkle in the rain!"

"Come back!" I yell. "I *am* a God outside the box, but we need to stay in the present if we're going to get anything done!"

Jesus and the Spirit reappear with me in space. "Okay!! Let's refocus. We are making **the beginning** here!! Be in the now and be present in the moment!"

I stepped back to observe.

It was missing something.

I was the first to speak to this new Earth: "Let there be light!"

Suddenly, a horrific intensity of light nearly blinded us! Jesus had to turn around to keep from being harmed from the brilliance of it all. I could see absolutely nothing but the washing white and yellow all around us, blurring my vision.

"Let there be dark," the Holy Spirit screamed.

And suddenly it was dark again. I felt dizzy having such a high intensity of changes so quickly!

"Whoa," I say, disoriented. "Jesus, can you do us the honors? Can you finish this up for us?"

Jesus said, "Certainly! Let there be light <u>and </u>let there be dark." He shouted to the nothingness.

Suddenly, there was a split. The one side of Earth faced a black hole of darkness while the other side was blinding light.

"Wow!! That's bright!" Jesus said, trying to cover his face.

"Okay," I spoke. "There will now be **day**. A morning and an evening. A day and a night. Time will pass. There will be a set time and a countdown to each day: 24 hours. That's 1,440 minutes and 86,400 seconds in a single day. That should be *plenty* of enough time to complete everything man needs to do. If that's not enough time, then he's clearly taking on *too* much."

The Holy Spirit opens the plan book. "Wait. I'm not seeing this time frame here. I think you have the time measurements during the Humanity Restoration Project. At this point, your creation will still be living eternally."

"Oh my. I *am* getting ahead of myself." I shake my head. "Yes. That is right! Right now, no *choice* has been made. My humans and animals were indeed created to live forever.

I then shouted the announcement that Night will be represented by this black darkness and Day will be represented by this bright light. Let this be marked as the very first day in history. Day One." I turn to the left and to the right. "What do you think?" as we stare at what we just made: a suspended ball of water illuminated by light on one side.

"I like it," the Holy Spirit said.

"It's very good," said Jesus. "I am happy we are starting this project. I remember when we planned this."

It all came back to me. At the beginning. No, the *very beginning*.

It was when the Heaven Project first started.

It was just me.

Well, me, Jesus and the Spirit.

And I loved our communion. I loved our togetherness. Our passion. Our drive. Our ideas for the future.

We agreed on one rule.

If we were to make a family...

If we were to start this process...

We have free will. So would everything we make!

We would love unconditionally, generously and gracefully!

We would be involved in our creation's lives no matter who they are. We wanted to be evident, obvious, personal and...needed.

We drew up the plans. We all signed at the bottom. We knew the risks. We understood the dangers. But we would be in this together and would stay with our creation...always...together.

We wanted a family!

And we started Heaven, making something out of nothing.

And now we are back at it again... starting another world from scratch.

"Let's go back," I shout, excited. "Let's see what our angels think!"

I get back and recognize the grandeur of Heaven immediately. "Hey! Look! They finished the pearly gates at the entrance," I commented as we pass through, feeling well-pleased with my staff. I am happy things are continuing to progress here without me.

The new light we *just* formed is still shining from the top and sides of my Kingdom, a light that had never been there before now radiated all around us. My glory is no longer needed to illuminate Heaven while this light is shining. My angels are looking up, pointing around them at the changes that had taken place. Some are dancing and my Seraphims are singing at the magnificence of such a spectacle. The day, as I just called it, is continuing.

I smile. My angels haven't seen anything yet!

I feel very emotional all of a sudden. I can't *believe* I get to do this. I can't believe *this* day is the start of **my** personal dreams coming true!

Luce comes up to me through the crowd and pats me on the back, "Hey, way to go! That's really bright!" He says. "Of course, I feel like that's **too** much light. Like, this new light can expose a lot."

"Expose? Like what exactly, Lucifer?" The Holy Spirit draws out his name. "By the way, have you thought more about the Palace plans? You know, we can always move you up, if that's what you want."

"Yes, I am working on it." Luce looks down. "And I didn't mean anything by it, just that the darkness can hide a lot. I guess I can't believe you got rid of it completely, that's all."

"We didn't get rid of it completely!" I say with delight. "There is now a day and a night. When it's nighttime, it will be dark around us again."

"Interesting," Luce commented. "Well, it's Day One. I cannot wait to see what happens the rest of the days! How long are you going to be doing this?"

"Seven. Seven days," Jesus said quickly, looking around and admiring the beautiful light.

"Then what happens after that?" Luce asks.

"It's going to take a lot out of us to create all of this," I say. "I'll sanction a day to rest. I'll need it for sure."

"*Definitely* some changes will happen after that," my friend smiles. "Maybe a promotion for someone?"

"Maybe..." I respond.

*****

"Ready to do this, again?" Jesus asked with excitement in his eyes. I notice Kailon and Agla talking to the Spirit about something. Angels have been steadily coming up to us confirming their tasks for the day and asking last minute questions, knowing it'll be late by the time we get back.

It was officially Day 2 and once again we all meet at the center of the Plaza surrounded by our angels.

"Wait, let me make sure I have both my keys." I look and see they are around my neck as always.

"Yes, I am ready." I breathe in deep.

The Holy Spirit has the plan book in his hand. "Let's go."

Up in space now, we circle Earth, looking at it intently. The Earth was still covered in water. The water started moving intensely as we arrive.

"For anything to live, we need to change what we have so far," I said. I then form an atmospheric shell around the Earth to protect it, calling forth a shield over my beloved planet.

I then call upon a split and suddenly the water divides and clouds, fog and mist leave the face of the Earth and rise up to hang above it.

I want this to be a vibrant and alive planet that will feed itself and work on its own. Water will rise and fall, a cycle of movement; water will rain down and evaporate up.

Like a painter, I step back.

We all three look at this forming blue canvas.

There was an obvious height, depth, and weight to this planet. The excited water was on the bottom and a thick layer of white clouds on top, moving around the sky slowly.

"And what do you call this top section of your Earth?" Jesus asked.

"I call it sky," I state proudly. "I want all my creation to be able to look up at something and see a powerful canvas of activity and know that I am responsible for what they see."

Earth still hung on nothing but space.

There was a large amount of outer darkness around the Earth.

"There certainly is a lot of blank space around here!" Jesus observed.

"In the coming days, I'm going to showcase my wonders over all this vastness so every living creature will know how real I am!" I shout.

"What do you say? Want to call it a day?" The Spirit looked at this barely touched new planet. I look at all of this and instinctively fiddle with my keys around my neck. There is still so much left to do!

I want to do more!

Jesus decides right then to wrap it up by saying "Yes. Yes. This is all good so far. Let's go back."

I nodded, restless but patient. It's best to leave now.

Jesus smiled and we head back to the awaiting crowd of angels. Kailon was the first to give me a hug, her blonde hair and sparkling eyes made me happy to be home. I noticed her friend Agla wasn't with her. At this point, the light in the sky was fading, marking the end of a day.

I did notice no more plaster was hanging from the west side of the Palace. I would be so happy if the renovations are complete inside! I'm sure I'll find out more about the progression of the Heaven Expansion Project during the Feast and Fellowship.

"You were up there all day!" The archangel Cassiel commented, arriving at the scene. "Everything okay? Do you need help! I would **love** to help!"

I touch him on his shoulder. "No. This is something I want us to do alone."

"Where is Lucifer?" the Holy Spirit questioned. "And why are so many angels not present right now?"

Jesus was leaving with some angels to go dine with them for dinner. He was clearly enjoying being back with his family.

The place was clearing out, leaving me and the Holy Spirit alone.

The Spirit and I share a glance.

"No. No *choice* has been made yet. I still have a lot for him. Nothing's been done, yet."

The Spirit had to comment. "But wait until he sees your Earth. I mean, he wants to rule Heaven so badly, it would be another place for him to - - -"

"I'll stop you right there!" I shook my head. "No *choice* has been made! As of right now, he's still on our side!"

The Spirit stared directly at me. "Are you in denial about the future? You know he's - - -"

"He's my friend! And I'm hopeful of the best. He wouldn't betray me. Why do you think of all the angels, I made *sure* to stay with *him* so closely? I made *him* special! I made none like him! I have <u>great </u>plans for him! So he could use his skills for good!"

"I know." The Spirit almost looked sad. "I'm sorry. I'm just prepared for anything."

"Well, get ready to be surprised," I said to him and, unknowingly, to myself.

Chapter 5

"**K**nock! Knock!" Luce popped his head into my office as I was just about to leave, his yellow eyes glowing. "Good luck today!"

I smiled. "Thanks! Hey, where were you yesterday? You know, when I got back? I didn't see you at the cafeteria later that evening, either."

"Oh, you know, taking care of some business."

"Any business I need to know about?" I ask inquisitively, patting my side pocket to make sure I had both my keys with me before I head out.

Luce bursts out singing: ♪♫♬ *"We are making a surprise for you! Because you are great! When this is all over, we will party on cue."* ♪♫♬

I laugh. I love his voice! "Well, thank you! Do some of the other angels know about this?"

"Oh yes! I have an entire section of *my* department waiting for instruction! I know it'll rock your world!" He smiled.

"I hope so! I love surprises! Remember when you planned that great song to celebrate the new worship wing? The entire choir got involved!"

"Oh! It'll be *better* than that!" He said "But you better hurry. You'll be late!"

"Yes, of course! I have to start my Day 3! But Luce, just remember...you can *always* stay here in Heaven. We can talk about you working directly under me."

"Really?" He asked.

"Sure! You can stay here with me."

"You know, I was hoping for a little more..." His eyes seem to be shifting as he said this.

"Depends on what you want, Luce. Do you want more? Or do you want to stay here with me?"

He was silent. I knew the *choice* was near. I had to be tactful.

But I also had to leave. I knew there would be another time to talk to him.

I rush out of my office with Luce and sprint to where the other angels were waiting for me at the center of the Plaza.

"Sorry, I'm late. We were talking!" I say, drowning out the noise of the crowd to the always punctual Spirit.

"We?" He asked.

I look around. Luce was nowhere to be found. "I was talking to Luce but I guess he's not here."

"I hear Lucifer's been pretty chatty lately," the Holy Spirit responded.

"What do you mean?"

"I - -- -"

"Come on guys! Are you ready??? Let's do this!" Jesus shows up all excited and pumped. "Day 3 awaits! Let's go!"

And with that, we quickly floated up like before.

I had a huge agenda to fill and I knew the angels were in good hands with the large group of archangels guarding them.

I look at my odd creation at this point. We had massive light still blasting into our eyes. We had the water now churning at our arrival at the bottom of this large sphere. This looks like a mess.

Nothing I can't work with.

"Okay," the Spirit reads from the plan book. "We need a section of dry ground so that this new creation can stand and live and be away from all this raging water."

"I can do that," I said. "I helped create a solid environment for my angels. I can create one for these new beings."

And with that, I called forth brown earth from inside of the shielded sphere. It came out from the water, rising from underneath, the strong metal core extending and rising, shaking the very foundations, creating vast spaces of land. A huge rumble of rocks piled together and pieces of land erupted into place. It was basically one massive piece of soil with water surrounding it on all sides.

"What do you think?" I ask, stepping away for a moment. "I want this brown area to be <u>land</u> and the water to be referred to as the <u>seas</u>." I bite my lower lip at the thought as if I was a sculptor examining his clay mold.

"Just so you know, time is going to eventually move that giant piece of land into different sections and pieces. Are you okay with that?" the Holy Spirit asked.

I thought for a moment. "Yes. That'd be fine. It will spread out my planet and use up all this space I have."

"I like it!" Jesus said, suddenly and instantly shrinking in size and now taking the very first step onto the new land, marking it as an official *Heaven-meeting-Earth* moment. He pats the ground with his hand, rubs it with his feet and moves around a little. "I think it's good. Solid. Stable. Forget Heaven, maybe I should live here!"

"Don't joke!" I smile, looking down at Jesus on Earth. "I made Heaven where **we** live!"

"It's not going to just be bare and barren, is it? Your creation can't just live on brown mud," The Spirit asks, flipping through the pages of the plan book.

"No. Of course not," I answer.

"Oh! This is where **I** shine!" Jesus said the only one of us who is standing on the ground on Earth. The Spirit and I are hovering over the planet and looking from a higher-up viewpoint, surveying the scene.

"I will make this Earth plentiful!" Jesus said. "It takes just one little seed." Jesus knelt down and something left his right hand and was buried into the ground.

"Tell us what you're planting," I say.

"Seeds from Heaven!" Jesus smiled. "This is *also your* holy place, is it not? I want the same amazing, plush, vibrant garden you have in Heaven to be here on Earth. We are going to sprout vegetation, plants, trees and flowers! This is going to be a canopy of goodness that will shout *your* name. The same beauty in Heaven will be the same masterpiece down here!" Jesus explains while digging seeds in the ground with every step he takes. "You want your creation to feel loved and overwhelmed by goodness? I can take care of that!"

Suddenly a large patch of land bubbled and shook and sprouted the most lush and plentiful looking garden, similar to the one I love and go to in Heaven. My Garden of Solace was now growing in front of me, only I will call this oasis something else...we all announced it at once...**Eden**.

A land of happiness and delight.

There was one tree that grew higher, further and richer than the others, one that had a waterfall forming at the top.

"Just a little touch from Heaven," Jesus smiled.

My Tree of Life.

It was beautiful!

All of it.

The massive garden just sang out to me as it grew! The yellows, the purples, the greens, the vibrant hues of red just rose to sing a melody of its love for me. Oh my! I was amazed. I was absolutely in love with all of this! It kept growing, spreading and expanding on its own. Jesus was getting lost in a plethora of majestic greenery! And all the while I was smiling and laughing.

"These plants should have seeds already in them, so they can form on their own," the Spirit was reading from the plan book.

"For now though, I also want to create an irrigation system on land," I suggest. "We will separate Eden into four paths from rivers that will feed these flowers, similar to the rivers in my Garden of Solace. This system will be used to produce food and resources as well as provide beautiful trees and fruit. The water will also feed my children as well."

This is going to work! This plan is going to work. I saw my vision starting to come to light. Finally! Some detail to this blank canvas!

I'm going to have **children**. I will call them each by name. And they will play, gather, talk and laugh in this fruitful metropolis I have made for them. I can almost see them now.

I cannot wait!

I hear Jesus laughing and moving, but I cannot see him in the newly formed mesh of plants.

This area is for **my** creation to live in. I will give *them* control on what goes on here. This will all be for **them**.

Jesus finally came back up to space, outside the Earth's sphere with bits and pieces of tree and leaves in his hair. He seemed out of breath and red in the face like he had been running and enjoying this little escape.

"I love it!!! This is all **so** good."

"Ready to get back?" The Spirit asked.

I looked at this landscape I have created, "Yes, I am ready for more."

✶✶✶✶✶

"Knock! Knock!"

I hear a familiar voice and turn around.

"Hey, Luce! What are you doing here?" I look up from my creation.

"I just wanted to visit you at work," he replied, nearly gasping at what he is seeing!

It was the official Day 4 and I was placing the stars just so in the outer realm. The Spirit was busy clearing out a vast expanse for the galaxies and Jesus was out somewhere forming the major planets.

"Don't touch the big yellow one! It's hot!" Jesus warns Luce as he is busy forming rings on one planet with a few ice sheets.

"I guess I can stop for a moment and give you the tour," I exclaim.

I had a bucket full of stars left to put up, but I guess that can wait.

"This will all be an impressive region for large objects and a glittery spectacle," I say pointing at the stars.

"Can I put up some?" Luce asked.

I nodded and started putting up some in a design of a square with a handle.

Luce grabbed some and started to copy me on a different area. "Oh! I can make designs? Wow!" He then created what appeared to look like a little dipper right near mine.

"And what is all of this for?" Luce asked.

"Well," I state, looking around. "Everything has a reason, but mainly I wanted something gigantic in the universe to show how big I am! But you haven't even seen the best part..."

I grab the plan book from the Spirit who was giving me a cautious look and lead Luce to Earth. To my beloved planet. The area where so much of my miraculous will take place.

"Here it is," I say proudly, the sphere moving in front of us.

"Can we see the scenic tour?" He asked.

"Come with me!"

I guide Luce down to Earth shrinking through the atmosphere. Luce was absolutely amazed and speechless!

Wow! The earth tickles to the touch and is so squishy under me. I touch a leaf and a branch. What wonder! I cannot *wait* to see what the angels think of all of this once it's complete. They will get to enjoy this world too!

I introduce Luce to the fruits that were developing and he takes a bite out of an apple. His face lit up! "So delicious!" He shakes his wings excitedly, feathers falling on the fresh soil. He snaps a nearby flower and looks at the broken lily petals in his hands.

"This fruit is like Heaven's. Truly marvelous!" He gasps.

I explained that humans and animals will walk around here. "Such greatness!" He exclaims.

"Thanks," I said, truly admiring my work. "I think it will all come together nicely." I then open the plan book to show Luce the animals we are going to make, flipping through to show the exotic colors, shapes and sizes of each animal.

"Wow. Stop right there!" Luce puts his hand down on a page and grabs a sketch from the book. "Exquisite animal..."

I look down and gulp. Luce seems to be fascinated with the animal crawling on his belly, its bright colors and fangs seem to be staring at us from the page.

"If you like bright colors," I suggest. "Then you would <u>love</u> these sketches of birds I am going to make!"

Luce kept eyeing the design of the snake as if attached to it somehow, as if connecting with it.

"This creature. It can eat an animal whole. It can squeeze its victims. It can latch on when least expected…"

"How do you know all this?" I ask.

Luce looks up at me, almost confused. "I don't know."

He gives me the sketch back and shakes his head as if trying to awaken from a daze.

"Well, I absolutely love all it! This is <u>perfect</u> for someone to rule over!" Luce said suddenly, almost instinctively. Almost surprised he said that.

"Yes. My boy, the one made from my very heart and soul. The first human being will rule over this all."

Luce stopped in his tracks, his feathers ruffled. "You've been promising me a promotion for a while now."

"But, you already rule so much of my kingdom, Luce! And I have something special planned for you. Just trust me!"

"You're giving all of this to a *newbie*?" He looked insulted. "Your human shouldn't get all this! I'm next in line!"

"Luce, I ---hear you. And listen…after the Creation Project, we can talk about your new promotion."

"Okay, but this discussion is not over."

"It never is," I mumble under my breath.

"I'm finished with the planets!" Jesus screamed as Luce and I enter back into outer space with the others. I spot all the massive orbs floating around, counting seven with a dwarf looking one in the back. "Is that one a planet?"

"I don't know," Jesus replied. "It's so small. Your humans won't even be able to see it. Oh! And over there I added more galaxies and more stars and black holes!"

Jesus turns to Luce who looked fascinated at the moon. "Oh yes. This one is *very* unique. This one will determine Earth's months and be lit at night from the sun." Jesus looked like he was demonstrating a show-and-tell to an audience of one. "Oh! And this sun will determine one year on Earth as the Earth moves around it."

Jesus was all giddy, showing Luce around the galaxy. "Oh! And over here! I created this big gaseous one to have heavy gravity to pull comets and meteors away from the Earth to keep them from crashing into it."

Luce looked impressed. "So, these stars, moon and sun will help create the seasons and days?"

"And even direction!" the Spirit quickly chimed in. He had been busy writing pages from the day and was now finally closing his notebook.

"Do you have shielding from this sun? It seems too hot for Earth," Luce had to know.

I walked him through this. "We made the magnetic field stronger; Earth is the right distance for life. Its speed of rotation is *just so*. The temperatures are *perfect* for the humans and animals to live. The pull of that moon and sun will create tides in the existing water so that oxygen can stay in the water thus the animals can breathe and keeps the oceans churning."

"I love how precise everything has to be," Luce added. "Like I said, this is a perfect place for someone to rule over..." The Spirit looked directly at me as Luce seemed to take notice that my keys weren't around my neck.

Of course, they were safely in my pocket.

*****

"Day 5 is going to be tough," Jesus spoke, shaking his head.

We were all three looking at the new Earth once again. The plants seemed to have done fine overnight on their own. The green, red and yellow flowers smile at us as we survey the scene from space.

"Why do you say that?" I ask.

"Because you're going to make animals today and I need to ask, do you even know how to make animals?" the Spirit consulted.

"I made everything this far, haven't I?"

"Yes, but you're talking intricacies of animals breathing on land, breathing on water, moving around on both land and water. This is a big undertaking. And look how much room you have to fill - - - -"

I interrupted the sensible, reasonable side of the Trinity. "Yes, but I am God. And I can do anything."

"I hope you have a good imagination," Jesus laughed.

I proceeded to leave the others and instantly shrink to walk once again on my lovely planet.

I get down to a crevice by a rock where I can maneuver my way down to the tip of the water (a small time ago I just called it *ocean*). I walk towards the water, making my way ever so slightly, inch by inch until I am waist down in the water. It's so cold! Everything in me laughs! This is an incredible sensation - to be out painting reality, forming another world altogether. I take out both of my keys from my pocket and put them around my neck. I don't want them to get lost in this endless stretch of water.

The sudden stillness of my new ocean makes me think maybe it knows something amazing is going to happen now that I have entered the scene. This nature truly knows me.

"To my ocean," I said. "I will give you the wonders of life."

I close my eyes and breathe in. I think deep as I escape into the wild imaginations of my mind. I reach back into a time when I thought about different kinds of wildlife. I thought about their fins and how they will move when they swim. I thought about their underwater gills and how they will breathe in the water. I thought about their diet, the seaweed, the coral, the reefs. I thought about so much.

I started calling to them. Calling them out. I felt the giant creatures leaving my imagination, manifesting out of absolutely nothing as it left my thoughts and then plopping right into the ocean, causing a huge splash in front of me. With my eyes still closed, I spoke into existence the long slimy bodies crawling and making loud noises as they make their entrance into the world. My eyes are still closed, but I could see them, every one, as they make their way out from my thoughts into the land of the living. I could hear them cry out as they entered reality. I could feel them swim and crawl and slither, all shapes and sizes, all color and all original, streaming forth life and abundance and beauty. They were all born for the seas! Their life is in the water. I created them with large tentacles, long noses, big teeth, and no teeth, small, with claws and some with just a large slimy body. All different and all formed completely from my creativity!

I finally open my eyes and take a large and exhaustive breath!

And smile so big!

Massive creatures in front of me are now playing with each other! Tiny sea animals circling bigger ones. Monstrous creatures are singing to each other in a tune only they can understand. They are all sharing the ocean in one peaceful play.

This **all** came from my heart, my mind, my spirit, my imagination and through the reality of me. They came from a peaceful place, a comforting place, a loving place and so thus they will continue to share that love with each other.

Everything I make has an internal knowledge of me, the reason why even the plants move toward me when I walk.

These animals will enjoy all this ocean I have made for them and I will love them completely. "You all play nice!" I scream as a friendly animal with a fin swims up to me, wanting to be petted.

"Hey! Look at this!" Jesus cried. I look up and he's flying along with a maroon- colored winged-creature up in the sky! The wingspan is massive! These creatures are causing a shadow where I am. What is that beautiful noise I hear? Singing! The birds are all singing a tune unique to them, so beautiful, filling the sky with an array of melody. They are just so happy!

"Wait! What?" I ask, quickly getting out of the water, dripping wet, shouting up at the activity taking place in the skies. "*You* made the birds for me?"

The Holy Spirit responded laughing. "You were taking care of the ocean. Jesus thought he wanted the sky!"

"I knew what you wanted!" Jesus screamed back.

"They're so cute! I love it!" I say. I get back to where the others were, all of us now in the sky admiring our handiwork!

Look at them! They are flapping their wings! They have rather large beaks. But what I absolutely loved was the creativity of each bird! One had a large neck. One was very small. One was bright orange, the other a bright red. They definitely looked like Jesus' handiwork; each made as original, colorful and playful as possible.

I extend my arm and a bat flies toward me and lands on my arm, content and happy to see me. I noticed he didn't have any feathers like the others. His skin stretched over his long arms. I noticed a different group of small winged animals fluttering together – butterflies, bees and bugs. They had thin scales to fly on.

I watched a hawk soaring, admiring his massive wingspan. These flight feathers are remarkable!

Jesus rushed to where I was, flapping his arms, nearly hitting me, laughing hysterically as he came to a sudden halt and all the birds and animals in flight flew past him in a winged frenzy! He was playing like a kid interacting with his new friends.

"So you just wanted to get credit for all of this?" I ask.

"Hey, I thought we were all in this together?" He replied.

"No. We are. You two are the only ones I trust with my creation. Make as you will," I said. I then shout down to the newly formed animals, "This is your land and water! Have fun! Be free! Fill the Earth with your abundance as you love each other. Cover this land with happiness and friendship."

"Can they understand you?" the Spirit asked.

"They know my voice," I reply.

"ArrrArrrr Rawwwwrr" Jesus said, acting like a large sea animal. I look at him. "What? Just trying to speak their language."

"Are we done? Can we go home now?" The Spirit asked, writing in his notes a detailed synopsis of the day.

"Thanks for letting both of us do all the work today!" Jesus teased the Spirit. "You just stayed up here writing your notes!"

"This is important," The Spirit responded. "Someone will one day read about Creation and I need them to know **God** did all of this. It will be the beginning of Chapter One of a book about you and your story to your people. It doesn't start with the angels and the Heavens though we have been here for a while. No. It'll start with the creation of your humans for the story is about you and your kids. From this Day onward." He then finishes writing and closes his manuscript. He looks up. "Sorry, so are we done here?"

"Not until you say it," Jesus implied.

I smile at Jesus' newfound humor.

"Say what?" the Spirit asked.

"Oh. *You know.* And we won't leave here until you do!" Jesus smiled.

An orange bird sits on my shoulder. I laugh and pet him as he coos back.

"Okay. I'll say it. It's *good*," the Spirit said suddenly.

"Now we can go back," I said. "To another day. And *that* much closer to seeing my kids!"

Chapter 6

We get back and I notice instantly there is a loud uproar in Heaven. Immediate tenseness hits me hard, an opposite feeling from my day of fun on the job. My smile is stopped as I see angels scurrying along, running and fleeing to and fro though it's coming on twilight. All of my order and structure in Heaven seems to be interrupted.

Something's not right.

"What's going on," I ask. The Plaza is completely empty. I can't find anyone to talk to! No one is waiting to greet us as we arrive.

Where are my archangels? Where's Luce?

"I'll get to the bottom of this," and with that, the Spirit disappeared, running in the direction of the angel bay. Jesus looked at me and shrugged.

"C'mon. Follow me," I say as I see angels shifting behind trees.

What's happening?

Jesus and I notice sounds coming from the orchestra room and we run in and sure enough, a large meeting is going on. Archangel Michael, Raphiel, Casandra and a few other archangels are up on stage answering questions to a full crowd.

They seemed to be overwhelmed and nervous. The atmosphere was thick and restless. The crowd seems to be criticizing any answers they are given. It seems some angels from before <u>still</u> have a problem.

"We should have more!" one screamed.

"This is so unfair!" yelled another.

"Do you think we want to take care of another species? We need to take care of ourselves first! We are not treated very well here."

Jesus looks at me with a worried look as we make our way quickly behind the wall and through the back corridor of the building.

I still hear their complaints, yelling their accusations about me not being good, not even letting the Archangels talk. The uproar of all these voices concerned me.

I find a back doorway and open it to reveal a place on stage. As we both come out in front of the light, the once loud audience is now silent as we approach the top of the stage and move towards the others.

I place my hand on Michael's shoulder and give him a gracious look and to the other archangels for holding down the fort for me.

"Do you want to stop progress?" I shout. "What is all this?"

"We were told you are being unfair to us!" one shouted.

"Who said this to you?" I ask.

"And you are putting too much work on us," said another.

"Where is this coming from?" I ask the crowd with no response.

I leave for *one* day and my Heaven is becoming a h - - -

"**I** told them," Luce interrupted my thoughts as he approaches the front of the audience, his tall stature undeniable, his massive wings stationed by his side. He seemed different. My *Morning Star* looks almost...darker.

Why does he look so different?

"Luce? What are you telling them? What is all this?" I ask.

"What you are doing is going to cause us more work." Luce looks directly at me and then speaks to the crowd, his back towards me. "And for what? We have a good enough system right here. Why add? Why are you even forming humans? Is it because you don't love us anymore? Are we second rate next to your *kids*? We were created *first*, you know! We should rule this new Earth together." Luce turned to me, approaching me with a scary look in his eye. I couldn't quite explain it. He seemed to be staring intently at the keys around my neck.

All of a sudden, the Humanity Restoration Project comes to me. The dark future I never wanted. Luce's betrayal. My family gone. A decision I never wanted to make.

I shiver at the thought.

No. This is not it. Luce hasn't made the *choice* yet. He's still with me. He's still here. I still have plans for Luce's promotion. It will be okay.

I turn to Jesus who was still beside me in the middle of all of this.

"Can you handle the crowds?" I ask Jesus gently. "Just answer their questions and reassure them that I love them. Don't let anyone leave feeling angry or resentful. Please deal with this for me."

Jesus put his hand on my shoulder. "I'm very good with crowds. I got this."

I then walk down the stage right to my friend and grab him by the arm. "Come with me," I whisper assertively.

I lead him out of the orchestra room and up and around the back, dodging the crowd.

I lead Luce to my office, away from the scene, away from the noise, just the two of us.

I open the door and the first thing I notice, my office is a mess! All of my drawers are open as if someone was looking for something! Chairs are knocked down, papers pushed to the floor. The golden safe where I keep my keys to the Kingdom is wide open showing an empty space! I'm happy I had both sets of my keys with me today.

Luce looks shocked and starts picking up items on the floor.

I know this is my opportunity to talk to my best friend one on one. I will use every chance I get to secure him to our side.

I pick up my chair, place myself behind my desk, exhausted from the day forming Creation and now coming home to find *this*.

I invite Luce to sit down as I rub my temples. What a *very* long day!

I look at my friend who is now fiddling with one of the awards I have on my desk. "Best Father to us all" it reads.

"Hey. Okay...*what* is going on?" I lean back in my chair.

Luce is silent, refusing to look at me.

Sensing his uneasiness, I ask delicately "What is it? You can tell me. In fact, I'm surprised you didn't come to me first. Why did you express your anger to everyone else in Heaven but me? We're closer than this, Luce!"

Still nothing. He just sat there, looking down.

"Luce. Please. What's going on with you?"

Finally, he looks up wide-eyed. "We can <u>rule</u> together! It's perfect. It's a perfect plan!"

"Luce, everything I do *is* for you! I gave you a prominent position! I created this amazing place right here in Heaven!"

"Did you?" He finally looked up, his yellow eyes appeared sad. "Or did you build it for *you*?" He shifted in his seat as if he's a guilty party on trial.

"Luce. I wanted a family. I wanted friends. For the longest time, it was *just* me. I had no one to talk to! No one to be with! And I created *you* special! I still remember it. When I created you, I called you *Morning Star*. You were so bright, more glorious than the others! I gave you extreme wisdom, favor, brilliance, beauty! I knew that I have created someone who could have the highest of positions! You were to guard my throne, to create musical masterpieces that would change the atmosphere of Heaven. You were to be such a close confidante to me. And you were! And you are! You're my best friend!" I smiled with such love and appreciation for Luce.

"Then why do you want a new family? Keep the one you have!" he said. "It's like you love *them* more than us!"

"I love you all the same, just different. You angels and this Heaven were my very first creation and I love you all! Your love and your adoration for me warms my heart and I love every opportunity I get to be with you!"

"Then why make - -"

"A new family? I'm getting there! I just wanted a new creation that I could call my own. You angels are independent thinking, this Heaven is so beautiful and this time is so precious. I just wanted to add to the family, certainly not take away. I wanted another creation that depended on me, that I could love and be loved in return, that I can help to be perfect and beautiful and full of brilliance, as well. You can understand that."

"I don't understand." Luce shook his head, putting my award back gently. "Because I don't have a place to call my own and people to rule over."

"Listen. Your problem is with *me*. Don't be telling all those angels out there that I am not good and that there is something wrong with me. C'mon! We can talk this out. We can fix this."

He started to smile a bit, acting like his old self. "Sounds good. But you know what would really make me happy?"

"What?"

"Assign me the position to rule over your new Earth!"

"Luce!"

"Do you not trust me?"

"It's not that..."

"Then what?? You love *that* boy more than me? More than your best friend?"

"Luce, stop."

"If we really are friends, you'd give me the keys. **I'm** the next in line." He gets off the chair, almost violently.

"Luce! Calm down! Tomorrow is Day 6. It's my <u>last day</u> of forming this new Earth. After that, I'm all done! And then we'll talk about your big promotion. I don't want to lose our friendship, you mean a lot to me. And I **never** wanted to lose any angels because of this new endeavor. I never want to jeopardize what I have here for what I am gaining over there. I don't ever want to lose you! You are <u>very</u> important to me! Luce, in the meantime, just...stay with me."

"Okay...." It was like he was processing what I was saying. I could tell a lot was happening in his mind, like a part of him wanted to trust me and another part wanted absolute control.

I smile. "Are we okay?"

"Yeah."

"Hug it out?" I ask, getting up and extending my arms wide.

He smiles and hugs me back, a sincere embrace. I definitely miss our talks together! And I do miss our time with each other. I didn't take into account that my absence may cause a dilemma here.

"I'll see you tomorrow?" Luce asks before he turns to leave.

"Of course."

Jesus comes into my office as Luce was leaving and stops him from exiting too quickly. "Are you okay?" Jesus asked Luce gently.

"Yeah. I'm okay," Luce answered back before leaving completely.

Jesus then walks into my office looking surprised at the ruin. "Whoa! What happened here?"

I shake my head at the mess.

"So how did it go out there?" I ask, going around the room and picking up papers off the floor.

"Everything's okay. I think someone or something just struck a nerve with those angels. Just some, not all. I can't even describe it. It's like they're fearful or worried about something." Jesus gets on his hands and knees to pick up some glass shards off the floor to dispose of them.

"Yeah, I think I figured out the culprit of all that," I sighed.

"Oh! Yes. How did it go in here?" Jesus asked finally, sitting down where Luce was, right in front of my desk.

"It's fine. We talked it over and hugged it out," I said, moving some spilled boxes before finally sitting at my desk.

"Do you think that helped? Do you think he's okay?" Jesus questioned.

I look down before I answer. "I don't want to lose him." I shake my head at the thought. "I can't lose him..."

"You won't," Jesus responded.

"You think?" I ask.

"I **know**. It's all part of his *choice*. To trust you or not."

"I keep reiterating our friendship and how much he means to me..."

"Then that should be enough. Anyone who loves you will stay with you, no matter what," Jesus stated.

"You're right. Where is the Spirit?" I ask, concerned.

"Oh, don't worry. He's handling the individual angels. He's actually at the angel bay right now, talking with them, spending time with them and just showing them how much we care."

"Good. Good," I relaxed a bit. "I appreciate you guys doing that. We can certainly do so much more and we can be everywhere when we work together like this."

"So, are you ready for the big day tomorrow? Last day! You get to finally meet your **kids**," Jesus announced excitedly.

I look away. "Am I doing the right thing?" I ask.

"What do you mean?" Jesus asked, surprised.

"I mean, *will* I be able to juggle Heaven and Earth. Was this too big of an undertaking? I don't want my angels to think I've forgotten them or that I don't love them."

"No. I would have told you if there was a problem with this plan. I think you are anxious because of what happened earlier. Don't let that stop you. You are <u>so</u> close to making your dreams come true!"

"Am I?" I get up off my desk and start pacing around the office. "My dreams coming true at the expense of what? *Is* this being created because of **me**? Am I just wanting more?" I stop and stare at the diagram of this project I made a long time ago now on the floor with a big X marked over Abigail and the man's face. I pick it up, upset.

"Listen. I know you," Jesus comforted. "You have *such* a big heart! You care so deeply for your angels and you love every single thing you create! I see you out in your Garden of Solace just smiling at the flowers who eagerly await your company! You're not doing this for you. You want to share your love, you want to be present in others' lives, you want to interact with your creation and you want to be known. You are the most compassionate being I know! You are willing to step out and do amazing things and if you were to ask me, you are doing everything for *them*. You are giving your old and new creation a beautiful place to live, bountiful food to eat, a grand fellowship and a Father who loves them. They have *every* opportunity in the world to respond to you and be close to you. If *they* don't see that, I don't know how else you can show them!"

"Okay, but answer me this. What if I arrive at my new Earth one day and there's chaos like there was just now? What if my people don't want me? What if they get mad at me? What if they don't trust me? I don't want to be ever sorry I made them!" I fiddle with my keys around my neck. I eventually take them off and place them on my desk.

"Well, that's for you to decide," Jesus explained. "We haven't made your humans yet. You can always decide before Day 6 if you still want them. I mean, you created a magnificent planet. I suppose you can always stop there if you wanted."

Jesus gets up off his seat and heads towards the door. "You're right. **True love** is a risk. You will risk getting your heart broken if you make another set of beings that have a *choice* to love you or not. You decided that you didn't want them to be programmed to love you; you *wanted* to give them free will. This is the risk you run into. What happened here, well, we handled it, didn't we? We had personal conversations and reassured our love for them. That should be enough even for your new creation, right?"

"Yes. I feel like it should be enough. I want my relationship with my kids to be enough, that I can be everything they need and that they will not lack any good thing," I respond.

"Then I think you're fine," Jesus said.

"Wait!" I scream, just realizing something. "A page from my Heaven Handbook is missing!"

Jesus shakes his head slowly. "Right on time."

I sighed. "Can you leave me in my office? I just want to think for a moment," I respond.

"Sure. Tomorrow's the big day." Jesus walks out before asking, "Do you want the office door open or closed?"

"Closed."

Chapter 7

The sun I made just a few days ago wakes me up from its powerful rays. I must have dozed off. I rub my eyes gingerly, trying to awaken. I was in my Garden of Solace. The daffodils smile up at me. I get up confused before I remember I went over here late last night. The sound of the waterfall and the noises of nature always help clear my head.

I had a vivid dream last night. I had a dream that my kids were calling to me. They were in the Garden of Eden that I created for them. They were *so* happy! The man waves me down; he wanted to see me. There were no boundaries between us. We had a very personal connection, so deep! I wasn't just their God; I was their teacher, their Father, their friend. It was a love I have never felt before.

Today's the big day. Day 6. The last day of creation according to my notes. I have a lot of ground to cover and only a limited time to do it.

I was so apprehensive to leave my spot in the Garden. Though I was excited to get ready, I knew the second I entered the center of the Plaza, it would be a bustle of angels wanting to see the new addition to the Heavenly family. And I will have to show them it's the right move.

This is the right move, right?

I saw the possibilities of the future, the growth, the vitality, the eternal love.

But if Luce makes his *choice* opposite of my plan, he will turn...he will do....I won't even say it.

"Hey! You're late!" The Holy Spirit commented as I strutted on the scene. Sure enough, the main Plaza was swarmed with angels and activity. It seemed the chaotic scene from last night had transformed into a wave of energy and excitement. Everyone knew this was **the** day as if everything else I had done merely set the stage for this new life to take place.

"Sorry. Where's Jesus?" I look around for him.

The Holy Spirit smiled and put the plan book under his arm. "He actually already got a head start."

We both lifted out into the galaxy and stopped right in front of the new Earth. It was brilliant as it had formed and developed on its own these past few days. The blue sky shimmered back at us, the white clouds whisked by in an artistic form. I breathed in the deep oxygen coming in.

"You did this," The Holy Spirit whispered. "You made all this possible. Remember that."

I smile and take a deep breath.

"Today's the day," I say out loud. "Day 6."

We both shrink and enter in through the atmosphere and we are greeted right away with massive amounts of green and multi-colored plants and flowers. I see my birds and sea creatures are still playing around with each other, forming a unity and a bond between their distinct groups. I believe those animals recognize me as I go nearer and closer to the surface for they stop and stare, moving towards the direction I am going. The birds seem to be following me.

The more I get to the surface of the Earth, the more I experience a shaking sound! I hear noises: squawking, squealing, mooing, baa-ing!

Suddenly, as the Spirit and I both stood on land, a rush of land animals came rushing at us! Small, big, HUGE creatures all ran to me. Some had four legs while others only two. I saw an animal with a hump on its back, one with a big horn on its head, another with a very large neck!

In comes Jesus, running with the animals, his face beaming as if he'd been chasing down this herd of wildlife for hours.

"Hey! Don't you love them?" Jesus asked, stopping towards us and picking up a small brown animal with two large ears and a fuzzy tail. "You took your sweet time getting up!" Jesus then unfolded a sheet from his pocket and gave it to me. "I went by the plans. I just used my imagination some." He smiled.

"Some?? I only had plans for a few animals! This is a hundred animal species!! Do they all live on land?' I ask.

"Yep, they sure do. Right down to that rodent next to you." I look down and two black creatures with large tails are staring up at me. "And they are all two of a kind. This big bunch of animals will keep getting bigger!"

"Wow. You *did* all this! I almost feel bad. I wanted to do this."

Jesus smiled. "Technically, you did."

"You know what I mean. Why didn't you wake me up before you started?"

"Because," Jesus looked very serious, puts his hand on my shoulder and stared at me. "Because I knew how important your kids are. And I knew you would want to devote the majority of your time today creating them *if* that's what you still want."

I nodded and smiled. I was very anxious to get started.

"Now, are you *sure* you want to go through with this?" the Spirit asked. "You've already created a nice place for all these living creatures and *they* will love you unconditionally."

"Yes, I'm sure," I say, trying to convince myself. "Jesus, keep the animals steady. I want to concentrate on this."

"You got it. Let's go gang!" and with that, he rushes off back into the forest with the rest of the creatures who seemed happy to follow, as if they were all playing a game.

"Okay." I feel *very* anxious now. I can't believe this is it. The moment I've been waiting for.

I planned this out a long time ago. I know just what to do.

I get to some wet red dirt near the water and get on my hands and knees. I sculpt out a form of a being that's been inside my heart for so long. I make the legs and the arms. I create spaces for his fingers. I smooth out the cheeks on his face and make sure there are holes for his nose.

All of this has been a dream of mine and here I am staring at a clay outline in the ground of a **man**. A million thoughts went through my mind. The possibilities. The potential. The hope. "Please don't let me down. Please love me," I whisper to him as I make him, my hands red from the clay.

"I'm right here when you need me," The Holy Spirit said, now getting on his knees next to me.

As I continued to mold the man, I realized he was going to have our characteristics and be made from our image. He will have joy, love, excitement, beauty and leadership. He is going to spread his knowledge and expertise into the world. I have set it up before time began for him to succeed! He would have *everything* he needs. I will see to it he always does!

"What do you think?" I stare at this clay figure before me.

"I think he's perfect," the Spirit commented. "What's his name?"

I turn to the Spirit. "You're the creative one in the group. You name him..."

The Spirit looked at the mold of the man like he was thinking. "Adam. I like Adam. Simple. He will be the first man of all men made from this red earth." I nod in agreement.

"Well, Adam. Let's make you live!" And with that, the Holy Spirit bent down and breathed into the man's nostrils. Suddenly a transformation started happening; his clay-like features were cracking and creating into a real form. The man was taking shape before my eyes: his head curving all the way back, his arm being raised from the ground, his shoulders moving around as the body lifted.

I was truly stunned at this sight. He was perfect! I knew the operations inside him were running smoothly: the blood flowing through his body, the organs working together, the brain sending signals instantaneously. He looked at me, his eyes blinking for the first time as he moved off the ground. I just melted! His look was amazing and his smile so bright! He seemed so thankful to be alive!

I turned to the Holy Spirit. I didn't know what to say.

"Speak from your heart," the Spirit nodded in my direction.

I held out my hand for this man to take. He kept looking at me from the ground where he was *just* made mere seconds ago.

I finally spoke, my voice trembling. "Hello...Son. I love you. I made you. I'm your God. I will always be there for you. I will do everything I can to keep you safe."

My love for him was so strong.

I made this man already programmed with language because I needed to be able to communicate with him. He's already mature with the ability to speak. I knew he could talk. I made him to be fully intelligent and fully prepared for this moment.

Instead...Adam just looked at me, intrigued. He then smiled and opened his arms in a wide embrace. I started crying, feeling his tight hold over me.

He then released his grip and said one word: "Daddy."

My heart grew bigger just then. That was it. That was all I needed to hear. The world, the universe, the air, and the ground he walks on...I'll give it to him. He can have it all! This place and all that belongs to it is *his*.

"You will always have me, Son." I tried to sound brave as I said this, but it came out more high-pitched and more emotional sounding than I wanted. I quickly wipe away forming tears.

Adam held out his hand as if he was intimidated by the wonderment of this new world and wanted to walk around but needed me by his side.

I cannot explain the immensity of love I felt for my Creation. I devoted myself then to be his God forever.

His hand held on to mine as we walked the land, the breeze blowing into our hair, the flowers gazing up at us as we pass. I wasn't even thinking about Heaven or about my responsibilities at the palace. I was truly thinking of nothing else but enjoying being in the moment with my Son.

I set the stage perfectly, all to his liking! I made sure everything was made first so that when he entered the scene, there would be nothing but beauty and majesty for him to adore. It was all for **him**! I pointed at the waterfall. Oh! And the fruits on the trees! And look! Look at that bird! Adam loved the birds; he would chase them just to watch them fly away!

Adam seemed to get ecstatic over everything he saw. He would turn to me and point at a funny looking animal with a long nose and laugh. He would scurry through the garden I made for him and lean against the huge tree trunk. He would pick an orange from the vine and taste it in his mouth, leaping in the air at such high enjoyment! It looked like he was loving every part of what I had given him. And I loved watching him be so appreciative of what I had done for him.

Though I made this land from scratch, I still wanted my kids to have assignments given from me personally to help expand my Kingdom. Every man will have a purpose and a reason for living. I had to make him useful to keep the Kingdom going.

In the cool of the day, I talked to him about how this world would be his. His job was to name all the animals. I felt like that was a good position for him, spending more time with this world he so loved. He could take his time, get to know all the animals and study their personality traits. I wanted him to think about each animal and personally name them as I plan on personally naming each of my children from here onward. Like father, like son!

At that instant, with such adoration for Adam, I took one set of keys from around my neck and I gave him the keys to Earth! I had one set of keys; he had the other. My set was for Heaven, his for Earth. He took them with honor, the gold GK reflecting up at him. His mouth opened wide! The weight of the world now belonged to him! Earth was all his and he was in charge of it. I didn't necessarily plan on doing this right then. I just wanted to; it felt right.

I saw Jesus come near us but was stopped by the Holy Spirit as the Spirit whispered something into his ear. Jesus nodded and walked away. The Spirit looked at us walking past and smiled.

I was nearly in tears every second. I wanted to be alone with my son. *Just a few more minutes of no interruption, please.* This is the best time I've ever had! Ever! This is the greatest thing that has ever happened to me: the role of a father. This child is truly my greatest gift!

I want the humans on Earth to meet with me regularly. They will see my face and hear my voice. I need them to know that I am here for them, with them and that I support and love them. That's my job, to handle all the needs of Earth and all the humans. It's a job I love and I take my role as friend, advisor and mentor very seriously! And now the role of father to this new breed.

Adam and I were walking and talking, soaking in the day until finally he turns to me and says, "One thing I want to ask?" He fiddled with his keys now dangling around his neck. He seems to represent me in so many ways!

"Of course. You can ask me anything." I said. The communication between us seemed unhindered and open the way I always wanted it to be.

"All the other animals have two kinds with them. A male and a female. I noticed them paired off. Is there another one of me? Or am I the only one?"

I could see there was a different look in his eye. Like he was alone somehow though I was right with him. "If there's not," Adam continued, "That's okay! I'll still be happy with what you have for me. I am <u>very</u> content here."

I knew my female counterpart would be a great surprise and gift to him, better than he could have ever imagined!

"Adam, my boy. Let's rest on this limb for a while. We've been walking a long time." Adam instinctively stretched out his arms and yawned, leaning over on the thick tree roots that were up off the ground. He then closed his eyes and seemed to fall fast asleep.

I knew Adam was in a deep slumber, and I zeroed in on his chest, his ribs. I knew he had several. Everything else I can't take away; he was perfectly formed to need everything I gave him.

We had to act fast. The Holy Spirit was right there, placing his hand on Adam's side, making sure he felt no pain during this operation. This all had to be painless and smooth.

I took one of his ribs and made sure his side was closed up as if he were seemingly made of clay again. I inspected my handiwork. Adam still seemed to be sleeping; he didn't feel a thing.

From the ground, with the mud and dirt, I formed Abigail. I made sure to put Adam's rib to connect to hers. I already had her look in mind. It would be the true counterpart to Adam. She would be everything he needed and more!

I fashioned her the same way I did with Adam. Two legs. Two eyes. One mouth. Two arms. Ten fingers. Ten toes. I counted them all. I gave her the same organs: heart, lungs, and ribs. Of course, she will always have one more rib than Adam.

But I thought about the female kind of the other animals. They were made to bear children, to be a life-giver, to be able to expand their kind into the world. I made sure this woman could do just that. She would have everything she needed to be able to bring life into this world. Adam and *her* will be one flesh and they will do everything together. Though I will be their God and I will love them and they will love me, there will be a rich closeness between the two of them that is more unique than anything else in this world and I will support and bless their union. Any children they have together I will also provide for and love continuously. I want this to be a generation and a family that I can be a part of for <u>all</u> eternity!

Quickly I worked. Thoroughly. Efficiently. Everything had to be just so; everything had to be just right.

I finished the last piece of her flowing hair and looked at her. Wow! She was the most beautiful thing I had ever seen! The Heavens, the Earth, the flowers, the sky....no! *She* is more radiant than anything or anyone I have ever made!

She will have my sensitivity, my compassion, my generosity, a loving and perfect counterpart to my son, Adam.

I didn't call on the Holy Spirit this time, as he was still attending to Adam's post-surgery. His hands were still on Adam's side, stitching up the area to perfection, making sure Adam was breathing normally and all systems were functioning smoothly.

This girl was truly an original and **I** wanted to wake her up myself. I put my right hand on her cold clay heart. With the power I had, I used my energy and force to awaken her. I could feel her heart pumping, beating, and pulsing. I could feel its power as I kept my hand there until finally, I released my hand and saw her coming to life before my eyes.

She awoke as if from a dream. She looked at me and it was as if she knew who I was. She seemed very self-aware, more than Adam was at the beginning. I could sense immediately that she had an air for adventure and wanted to explore. She got up and touched the Earth under her. She picked up a nearby flower in awe. She started moving towards the sounds of creation around her.

But she wasn't going to go off running. Not just yet.

She noticed Adam sleeping on the ground nearby. She stares at the Spirit beside Adam. Though he's invisible to her, it's like she knows he's there somehow. She goes to where Adam is and tries to wake him up, gently shaking his body. She knew he belonged to her, that they were made for each other. I watched this scene unfold before my eyes. It was amazing to see the very first interaction between two humans. Ever.

The more I imagined her role, the more I realized...she wouldn't just bring *me* joy. Her job isn't to bring *me* joy. I looked deeper at her – her beauty – her position – her strength – her power. She has a greater purpose. She would bring life to this whole Earth. It would begin with *her*.

Another name came to me. Right then. Right there. I looked at her and said "She is the mother of all life. And she will continue the human race." I said. "Her name will be..."

"Eve!" Adam woke up and his eyes became wide with surprise and his smile was the biggest I've seen it! "Your name is Eve! It's you! I wanted you!"

Adam touched her face and stared into her eyes like he already knew her. He instinctively reached for her hands, her shoulders, and her face. It was a look of captivation that not even my entire garden could provide. He was entirely smitten!

I felt a hand on my shoulder. It was the Spirit's. "It's time to go," he whispered. Jesus stood next to him now, on his shoulder sat an animal with a long tail.

I watched as Adam and Eve talked and walked, hand in hand, pointing out their surroundings, getting to know this new world together. Such a sweet sight!

"Wait. Before we go," I said honestly not wanting to close this precious time but I knew the day was coming to an end. "I have to leave them something."

"But you have already left them everything," the Spirit said.

"I have to leave something here for them for their *choice*. Otherwise, I've set it up for them just to love me and I don't want that. I want them to *choose* me."

"Are you *sure*?" the Spirit inquired. "Think about what you're saying. That means they might not *choose* you."

"We decided this back when I made my humans and the angels and I'm not turning back on that decision now! In order to have their love, I want **all** of their love, no question!"

Jesus finally spoke. "Is it something in the Garden you will decide as their *choice*? I would hate for you to curse something in such a wondrous place."

I looked around. I saw trees and animals and greenery! Their *choice* had to be obvious, had to be available, had to be forbidden.

Towards the middle, near the Tree of Life with the huge waterfall, I grew a regular-sized fruit tree. Nothing was wrong with it; it looked perfectly normal. It was similar to all the other trees in Eden. If anything, this one looked simple and out-of-sorts with the rest of the magnificent garden. There was nothing poisonous or tempting about this tree at all. But unfortunately, I had to curse this tree, the one thing I have ever made that was cursed. It was *only* cursed because it *had* to be; it was their *choice*.

To make it obvious that is was <u>the</u> tree to stay away from, dark clouds started to hover over it. This lonely tree seemed like an outcast from the rest.

Adam and Eve could *choose* me and do what I tell them or they could *choose* to walk away from me and eat from <u>this</u> tree. I didn't even make it look tempting! There were tons of wonderful and delicious, more delightful trees they could eat from!

My kids looked at the cursed tree and didn't even seem interested.

In my perfect plan, they would never go to that forbidden tree on their own. There was no reason for them to disobey me.

Adam was busy showing Eve the keys I gave him, both holding such high authority in the palm of their hands. I knew they didn't care about what they can't have. They were too full of my goodness! I knew they wouldn't eat of that tree. I just knew it. I was confident in this!

Before I left, I gave Adam and Eve <u>one</u> command. That was it. Just one. Do not eat the fruits from this forbidden tree or you will die. I had to be all dramatic in this warning. It was for their own good for them to not have what is not theirs to take. If they ever did...it would be the end of this amazing, unfiltered, unhindered life *we* have together.

I would never want that to happen!

It was all set up to be their *choice*. That's how I knew that they would love me unconditionally and want me forever. I had to take that risk!

"Do you want me to put up signs around this place to remind them to stay away from this tree?" the Holy Spirit inquired, the one who always wants to show signs as a reminder of my laws.

"No," I respond. "I want my words of warning to be enough."

That was it. I made one final announcement. "Just stay away from that one tree from the rest of the trees in the garden. Other than that, enjoy yourself to the fullest!" My kids and I hugged and kissed each other, promising them that I'll be back to check up on them very soon!

Day 6 complete. And it was *oh-so-good*!

I needed to rest now. I got back up to Heaven exhausted as the day was coming to an end.

We had made the heavens, and Earth, the stars and the animals and all living things. I needed a break! And I needed one on my Day 7!

Chapter 8

It was now dark and quite late by the time we got back to Heaven! I could see the fine lights of the beautiful palace glittering at me. I could feel the weight of the world just fall off my shoulders as I get to familiar territory. Home.

Wait! Oh my!

The palace looks bigger. Brighter. No more plastered-up walls!

A huge portrait of me is showcased in front of the palace just like I had requested!

The palace is *finally* done!

Wow!

I get down and Gabriel greets me. "Sir. Heaven to your specific orders is <u>complete</u>."

I am truly stunned! I am completely losing it! This is all *so* overwhelming!

The massive palace with its tinted silver lining, the twelve gates at the entrance covered in pearl, the streets glittering in gold! I love it! I absolutely love it! No more construction! No more tarp or plastic covering. It's **all** done!

It is ALL SO good!! I was getting emotional all over again!

Each of the Godhead signed off on the bottom of the Heaven Handbook to officially state that the Heaven Expansion Project is complete. Well, for now.

I know Heaven is massive, so only a small bit of the space has been completed. But for now, let me marvel at what has just taken place. Let me stop and appreciate all the hard work!

I look past Heaven at all I have created. The planets are rotating like they should. The moon is casting a white shadow on Earth. The sun is a giant sphere of heat. I am truly in awe at what I have formed... from nothing.

I am so weary but so thankful. I feel so loved. I have a family on Earth <u>and</u> Heaven and now a home built for kings.

*****

I rested on my Day 7. I wanted no one to bother me and I was taking no conferences, no scheduling, agendas or meetings today. Just. Not. Today.

I made this day **holy**. For those who work as hard as I do to make their dreams a reality, I want them to rest on the seventh day. I want them to re-gain energy and strength; it will only benefit *them* to keep going.

I wanted to be left alone. I escape to my quiet area, on top of my holy mountain to just look up in amazement of all I had done the past week, the beauty of Heaven behind me. What was once an empty vastness of nothing now held color, power, and wonder!

I deem everything perfect and beautiful and so good!

I wonder what my kids are up to.

My heart was completely focused on getting to know my boy and girl more and how I *long* to play such a large part in their lives. I'm sure they are having a great time together! I can't wait to visit with them again and walk with them in the cool of the garden!

I sigh. I can't believe it. My dreams have <u>officially</u> come true. It only gets better from here!

"Knock! Knock!" sounded a familiar voice. "Need some company?" Sure enough, Luce approaches me. He seemed to be in good spirits.

"How did you know where I was?" I asked, moving over for him to sit next to me.

"A God going M-I-A for the day? Easy to figure out." Luce sits down. "Congrats by the way. This all looks amazing. All of it. You did a great job."

"Thank you," I said, still looking out into the vastness of my creation. "I am **in love** with my kids! No! Luce! I mean, I am **in love** with my kids!" I shake my head in disbelief.

"The wonders of the galaxy and all you can think about are those humans?"

"I feel such a deep devotion to taking care of these kids and being so genuinely close to them, you know?"

"Actually, I don't know. I am not able to create anything myself. But I'll take your word for it."

There was a little bit of silence between us before Luce starts us again. "So, are you going to assign anyone to watch over these new creations? Give someone more title or position to manage over the humans you've created?"

"No. They'll be completely mine. And only mine. I want the direct privilege to watch over this Earth closely myself. If I need help or angelic backup, I will call for it."

"If the world you created is perfect, then why would you suggest that you may need help?"

"Well, Luce. My plan has a risk involved."

"Oh?"

"You see, my kids are allowed a *choice* to follow me. Similar to all you angels here. Your *choice*, of course, is the keys. I manifested my kids' *choice* in the shape of a tree. It's a simple tree. There is no way they would wander to it on their own and absolutely no way they would want to eat from it, especially not since the other trees and their fruits look so delicious. But I had to include that forbidden tree in the garden. I didn't want to. But I knew that if they didn't have that *choice*, then I wouldn't be loved by them unconditionally and that's all I really want. That's all I will ever want from them."

"What happens when they eat of this forbidden fruit?" Luce inquires.

"No. Not *when*...if." I corrected. "IF they do, well, they'll be lost from me."

"Interesting. Hey, I thought you had two keys?" Luce asked.

I looked down at the set of keys dangling around my neck. I was hesitant to admit, "Oh! I gave one to Adam. He's in charge of taking care of the entire Earth."

I waited for Luce to make a big deal, to throw another tantrum...but he said quite calmly, "So that's official, huh? Interesting."

"I guess we need to go." I turn to Luce.

I am not really ready to get up and do anything but the Spirit is having a big celebration and Jesus is giving a speech. It's all arranged. And of course, I am the main event. It's to unify us as rulers of the entire Heavens and this new Earth.

"Are you happy with everything?" Luce asked as I was getting up. He was still sitting there as if staring out into something.

"I am. Aren't you happy?"

"Happiness is giving orders, making decisions, having others follow you. I don't have any of that."

"What do you mean?" I was surprised at his answer. "I put you in charge of the musical choir! I gave you the greatest position of guarding my throne and thus *my* personal holiness!"

"Did you? I would **love** to rule over something you've made! I'm asking you nicely, one more time. I know you want to personally guard over your new loved ones, but you can trust *me* to take good care of them. And then I will feel like I am *really* in charge."

"C'mon Luce. Come with me to the party. Remember your big promotion I have planned? Just trust me. You'll like it!"

"I don't want to." Luce seemed to be overreacting in a way that seemed nearly defensive. But I knew I had more time to talk to him now that this big project was over. I know he was upset that he didn't get what he wanted, but Luce's Promotion Project is next. I know he'll be pleased with that!

"Fine. It would mean a lot to me if you came. Just... stay with me. I'll make sure to give you what you're requesting." I said walking past him. "Right now, I have to go. I'm already late."

"I'll try to make it," was his weak reply.

*****

"And this is all thanks to our leader and ruler, God Almighty!" Jesus screamed out. There was a thunderous applause from all my staff giving me a standing ovation at the newly renovated Dining Hall.

It was massive! So much more space! The decorations of gold and silver trimming lined the sides and the back of the room.

This was <u>such</u> a monumental moment! This was truly a dream for me to be here. Not only was a new life taking place but my former creation was excited about the possibilities. I'm so happy I started this! I am so happy I followed my heart!

"Thank you! I am anxious to show everyone around," I yell at my family. "The new heavens look amazing. Feel free to fly around and explore what I have made! Thank you all for your fantastic help with the Heaven Expansion Project! Construction was long and tedious but you did a tremendous job. Doesn't it look *Heavenly*?"

Another loud applause erupted.

"So this part is for you! Let's celebrate the start of this new beginning!"

"And now," Jesus announced, ending my speech. "Enjoy the banquet."

I came in late so I didn't see the massive amounts of food until just now. Desserts, treats, culinary dishes on massive plates were being carried out to the angels. Everyone looked so delighted. I saw them all, all the archangels, all the worship choir, all the construction crew, everyone getting along and ecstatic to be together in this fellowship.

All but one.

I didn't see Luce.

Chapter 9

"**W**ake up!! Wake up right now!!!" I hear the Spirit's desperate plea.

What - - I hear screaming coming from outside my door and repeated loud knocking.

Suddenly, as if a grip of death started to choke me, I had a feeling that something had gone terribly, horribly wrong as I was resting.

Like a madman, I leap up and grab the door and open it to a sight I have never before seen!

It was dark. Panic-stricken angels were screaming and running for their lives.

The Spirit grabbed me on my arm. His look was of pure terror. "I knew I never trusted him."

"Who? No...No..." I couldn't wrap my mind around what was happening. "When? How? Is it? It can't be." I stutter.

Was this it? The moment I never wanted to happen...

"It's your supposed best friend," the Spirit kept me informed as we moved. "In the middle of the night, he plotted with all those who serve under him. They have been revolting, protesting against the Kingdom. Apparently, he's been telling other angels that you are being unfair, that they should have more, that they should be treated better." In the frantic rush of the run, I saw my Heaven vandalized. Rule signs were knocked down. My garden was a mess, piles of rubies smashed. I hear horrific screaming in the background. The areas marked GK were X'd out and now had LK written on them.

I saw my giant portrait at the Palace now in pieces on the ground and Lucifer's painting from the orchestra room was put in its place.

The Spirit continued to grab my arm and nearly dragged me as we ran together, but this time through secret passageways, away from the chaotic scene taking place, through hidden doors and narrow hallways. The Spirit seemed to know where he was going. I was still in a shocked haze.

"There's a fight going on. It's been brutal. Lucifer has about a third of the angels with them and they are strong-willed. It's like they have something to prove. It seems Lucifer wants **you**."

"Where are they?" I ask.

"Michael and the other archangels are fighting. They are in the outskirts of Heaven near the gates. He wants to go down to your Earth. They're powerful, strong! Jesus took the lead and is with them now."

This can't be happening.

The Spirit instantaneously looked down at the keys around my neck.

"I think I know...exactly what he wants!"

I shake my head. No. I was just with him yesterday. No. Not him. Not....

I just need time with him. I can make this all better. Just give me time!

"Jesus and the archangels are fighting back. I'm going to go help."

"I am too!" I insisted.

"We got this. We need you here."

"I can't just sit here!"

And with that, the Spirit rushed into one of Heaven's tucked away interior rooms and nearly pushed me into this vacant cell and I was alone.

I was shaking hysterically.

Why didn't I fix this when I had the chance?

My heart is breaking - for the first time ever - my heart is literally breaking! I had a hard time breathing. My chest was in pain. I felt dizzy and couldn't seem to stand.

My kingdom! My angels! What did I do? What didn't I do? All the thoughts spiraled around my head.

Nooooo!!!

I lost him. Could I have done something? Is this my fault?

I cling to the side of the wall for support.

My head is spinning. This can't be real. This has to be a nightmare! Please wake up!

He had his *choice*. I know he did. But I didn't want - - I never intended - -

Is this *my* fault?

I pace around the room, the tears frantically falling off my cheeks. I know what is going to happen. I know what the next step is. But I can't. There is a *choice* in Heaven. And Lucifer made his decision.

Rebellion can have no place in Heaven. But now I need to think of what to do. Can't I just talk to him? Maybe I can reason with him.

A very long time had passed and I sunk myself in a spiral of despair over the events taking place, something I knew would bring a terrible wave of great change.

Finally, I hear a sound. The Holy Spirit opened the door, slowly, a very large frown on his face. He looked...disappointed. He led me out of the interior maze and out into the open Plaza. He seemed out of breath, updating me as we walked. They had captured Lucifer and his band of followers.

"The others are tied up outside. We have arranged the procession trumpets to sound at your command," the Spirit reported back.

I look and a part of the worship choir with their trumpets were on the scene. They were shaking and scared, not sure why they were called for such an occasion and not sure why their friends were tied up.

The Spirit asked them to play their trumpets and they did, not realizing the true extent their final notes would bring.

I shake my head. "No. I can't."

The Spirit looked at me, determined. "There is no rebellion in Heaven."

It looked like Michael and the other archangels had been through a rough battle; beaten up, feathers everywhere and white robes soiled.

I look at Luce.

I knew that if I can't talk him out of what he's doing...if I can't convince him to stay with me...then I'll lose him *forever*.

I walk to where the rebels are tied up by the archangels. Wow. This was *some* fight.

I am literally shaking. So angry. So hurt. So betrayed.

I look around and the Plaza shows other angels scared, some hiding. Kailon is screaming at Agla who is tied up, begging the other not to do this, to stay with her, to be with her.

What has caused so much division?

The Spirit starts to form an area of darkness. It's far away from Heaven. I can see it developing. The Spirit is making the place full of fire, despair, loss; the temperatures will scorch and torment the rebels for all eternity.

I shake my head. I can't. I can't.

Tears are just running down my face. I can't do this. I can't.

I look at all those tied up. I look at these angels who live in my Kingdom. I know their names. Hanasiah helped build the roof on my palace. Kushiel fixed up my Garden for me. Mebahiah is the chef in the Main Dining Hall. I look out. There's too many. I can't send them all. I - -

I turn to look at Luce who refuses to look at me.

Luce looks **completely** *different* than when I saw him just a short while ago. He was dark in his appearance. The once great *Morning Star* looked like the light had all burned out. I didn't recognize him! This was definitely <u>not</u> the angel I formed. Here stood before me was something *he* must have created, something *he* must have wanted. His yellow eyes, his once brilliant eyes of gold, were now a burning yellow with a pursuit of power.

"Okay," shouted Jesus, all roughed up from the fight and now watching the Spirit form *Shoel* – a place of unending torture. "When the 5th trumpet blows, the doomed will meet their fate."

The rebels who were tied up saw what was waiting for them. The other angels around them in the Plaza had no idea what we were staring at...what awaited their fallen friends.

Why would anyone want to leave a place like Heaven for a place like...that?

Why would anyone *choose* that?

No. No. I'm running out of time. Please. No.

Luce and the others will leave Heaven so fast and all of the captured will be stripped of their beauty, their positions and their rights to Heaven. Once the 5th trumpet sounds....

The first trumpet blew. The first in the succession. The sound pierced my heart and rattled my nerves.

"Luce. Please. Please. Let's talk about this," I pleaded, turning my attention to the one who started it all, dirt and muck dripping down his face. I knew that once the 5th trumpet sounded, I would never see my friend again. This is my last chance for him to come back to my side. Tears welled up in my eyes. If he doesn't turn back, if he doesn't *choose* me...

I can't lose him! I can't send him to that horrible place! Not him – he knows me too well! He's been with me and close to me, expanding my Kingdom. He's made me laugh; he sang to me. Please, not him!

Tears were now streaming down my face. "Why? Please. Just tell me *why*?" I ask as I look at the angels I love chained up and tied up, beaten and bruised.

Finally, Luce spoke. He stared at me with an acute coldness in his eyes. "You don't get it, do you?" spitting out dirt and struggling with his hands tied back by Michael. "It was a wonderful plan. The first time I saw your Creation, I loved it. It's brilliant. It's **exactly** the kind of world I saw myself ruling over. I have great plans for your *kids*. If I can't rule Heaven, then I want Earth."

A 2nd trumpet blew its sound. My heart was sinking. Jesus was watching me closely as he, Michael, Gabriel, and Raphael held on to the rebellious angels by the ropes.

The Holy Spirit nodded as if confirming what I needed to do.

Now the 3rd trumpet sounds.

I visualize the fate that awaits these rebels. I see them turning over and over in their fiery grave, unable to die, just being massacred by the waves of horrid nightmares, blaming me for their fall. Wondering why I didn't love them.

I do! I do! That's why I'm begging them now! It's a place without my presence. They would be trapped forever in the midst of dark agony unable to leave.

The 4th trumpet sounded.

One more to go.

I was desperate. I turned to Luce one last time. "Please. Don't do this. *Choose* me. Please, Luce. Remember the good times we had? Remember our friendship? I am *begging* you. Stay. Stay here with me. We can work this out. We can figure this out. I have a promotion for you! You were next in line!"

"I am going to rule your Earth," He replied, unwavering. "Just wait and see. I will take your *precious* family away from you. I will **finally** have followers. They will **serve** me in everything they do. And I will be a more effective ruler than you! You'll watch as I take from you everything you love." He snarled. "And if you come to stop me, I'll make my followers kill you!"

"I know the future, Luce. It's terrible for you. Stay. Take the Promotion! Work under me." I plead.

"I don't want to work under you." Luce's eyes stared into mine. "I see the future, too. I see servants. Your people following me, preferring **me** over you."

I stare at him as he's talking. I know he hasn't been to the end and back as I have. But he has certainly caught a glimpse of things to come...

Finally, the 5th trumpet blew. I walked away as Luce attempted to reach for my keys only to be pulled back again by Michael.

"You did this, friend," Luce growled. "You couldn't have just promoted me like you <u>promised</u>."

"No...Luce. You *chose* this," I whispered, unable to form words. "If only you knew what I had planned for you."

"Just answer me this. Why *him*?" Lucifer spit at the thought. "What does *he* have that I don't?"

"Me," I spoke firmly. "He has me."

The Holy Spirit came to Luce and looked him right in the eye. I can't believe this is happening! "You will no longer have access to Heaven. You are stripped from your title and your position. Your name is no longer Lucifer the *Morning Star* but Satan, *the adversary*."

The Spirit went down the line, informing all those tied up where they were going.

I was trembling.

He then turned to look at me.

I can't do it. I can't see my loved ones suffer.

I can't just cast out my angels as if they mean nothing to me!

This was **never** my plan. This was **neve**r what I wanted!

I suddenly thought about the angels <u>still</u> loyal to me. I thought about my family down on Earth.

I thought about Adam and Eve's smiling face.

To save those I love, I must...

To honor their *choice*; these rebels clearly don't want me and they want to be away from me...I must....

With tears streaming down my face and a painful, heavy heart, I turned my back on one-third of Heaven and my best friend and said the words, "Be gone from me."

I couldn't watch it, but I knew the once-angels disappeared in a blink of an eye. They were cast from Heaven so fast, like stars falling. The haunting song Luce sang as he fell. ♪♫♬ *"The keys to Earth will be mine! All mine!"* ♪♫♬

It was quiet like nothing had happened only I knew in that instant, everything had changed! And my Kingdom was unraveling at the seams.

"Nooo!" Kailon screamed! "Where did he go?? Where did they go?"

The remaining angels went to the spot where their friends were once standing.

They were screaming, reaching, looking around for their loved ones, distressed they couldn't find them.

"He's coming back! He's coming back, right?" Kailon screamed with tears in her eyes.

"My friends!" Another cried!

"Where did they go?" Another yelled at me!

I fell down on my knees. My body was shaking with grief.

How could this have happened? I keep asking myself over and over again.

Was I not a good God? A good boss? A good friend?

I don't know what I could have done differently.

Did I not provide everything my angels need and want?

Could I have done better?

Am I a bad God?

Quickly, I get up in a panic and turn to my most trusted allies. The archangels with sadness in their eyes are collecting the ropes they just used to hold the rebels. I shout anxiously, "*He knows everything*. He knows about my kids. He knows their weaknesses! Oh no! He knows about their *choice*! The Tree. He knows Adam has the keys! He's going after Adam! He can't right? He can't - -" I yell insanely.

"Calm down. I know how much they mean to you." Jesus looked down with sad eyes and then said very slowly, "I'll do it. We planned for me to go down, remember? I'm going down to Earth. I'm leaving Heaven. I'll get our kids. I'll walk among them. I'll leave Heaven to save our family from *the adversary*. I'll make sure they come to you and *choose* you. I'll give them the opportunity to never be away from you so you never have to go through this again...never seeing your loved ones fall again."

I knew he'd say that. I knew he was ready.

I wasn't ready...

I can't see more of my Kingdom divided. And just thinking about what is going to happen to Jesus on Earth!! No...!

I know we planned this, but I didn't want this. I didn't intend this to happen. Not like this! I had worked so hard on Luce's promotion! It was going to be after Creation was made. Luce was going to stay.

...He was going to stay here eternally.

And now he's...he's...

"We knew *choices* were going to be made. You knew this was a risk," the Spirit spoke, a harshness in his tone.

"Not now."

112

"You knew this could happen," he said again.

"Stop," I stared at him with a tense look in my eye.

"BUT we made a plan. We have the Humanity Restoration project right here! We'll restore this. We'll fix this. Everything will be fine!"

"LUCE IS GONE!" I scream.

"THAT WAS HIS *CHOICE!*" The Spirit yelled back.

"This hurts. This hurts. You can't even...."

"I can't even what?" the Spirit questioned, getting close to me. "You think this doesn't affect me, too? I lost friends today. I lost them **forever.** You think you're the only one in pain?"

"What do we do?" I ask, feeling defeated.

"We have to keep moving forward! That's all we can do. We already lost some of Heaven today. Let's not lose Earth, too."

I turn to Jesus. "I can't. I can't ask you to do this. I did this. I have to fix this."

"No." Jesus was insistent. "I volunteered. I signed up a long time ago to live among your people so that everyone who lives on your Earth knows about you and *how* much you love them."

"Okay. First things first. We need to rebuild," the Holy Spirit said looking around at the desecrated Heaven. "We need to be able to defeat *the adversary* at his own game. He needs to know Heaven is not to be messed with! He knows our game plan. We need to set up a strategy so he won't suspect our attack. Michael, you're taking over for Lucifer. You have his position, now. Cassiel, you're on security duty! We need help. We need angelic backup. Angels, you are now strictly assigned to Earth. Jesus, when you get down there, teach these humans how to call on angels if they need them. Station angels on all four posts at the gates of Heaven."

I looked out into the sky, past the planets, past the moons, through the Earth and down to where Adam and Eve were playing. I saw something crawl up to them. It had yellow burning eyes immediately going after the keys.

"What is that?" One angel shouts at the new activity happening. "Did you make that?"

"It's a twig. A stick." One archangel commented.

"No. No, it's moving!" another screamed. "It's hiding. It's camouflaged by that forbidden tree."

"No. Leave my kids alone! No!" I screamed. "Noooooooo! Adam, guard the keys! Daddy's coming, kids! Daddy's coming!"

Jesus shakes his head. "I'll stop him!"

"No!" The Spirit said quickly. "It's Adam's *choice*."

"But it'll ruin everything!" One angel pointed out in dismay.

"It'll ruin nothing," the Spirit assured. "We have a plan of Salvation. Of restoration. Of reconciliation. But we have to move quickly. God, sign off on the Humanity Restoration Project. We are not going to do this without you. Just sign it so we can move on. The Creation Project is officially over."

"Can you give me a minute?" I ask. "Just a minute."

"Of course."

"It will work right?" I'm shaking as I speak.

The Spirit eyes Jesus who is comforting nearby angels. "We have a backup plan."

"Keep reminding me that."

"Trust me," were the Spirit's final words of the night. "It will work."

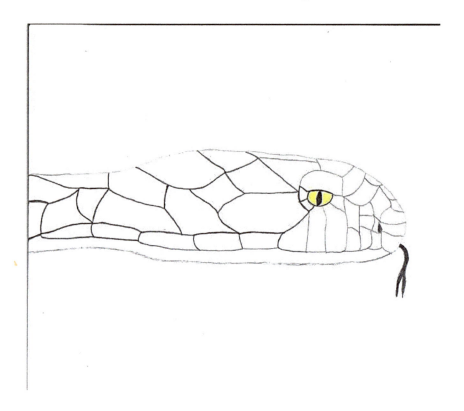

EARTH ~~Heaven~~ Handbook

Creation Project

God's Kingdom

CENTERED AROUND ME

~~OK~~ LK

Article VII : Heaven's Regulations and *The Choice* for the Angels

Section III : LUCE'S EARTH !

Heaven is a place of true worship, designed to be a home for God and his angels. The angels can come and go as they please. These free moral agents have access to every room, area and place in Heaven while completing their tasks for their divine assignment. The Creator in Heaven agrees to provide luxuries for such beings and make sure all of Heaven and all its operations are running smoothly.

MY ANGELS WILL HAVE FREE REIGN !

In the unlikely event an angel wants to discontinue being functional in their task or start in with behavior contrary to his primary role, as a preliminary option, several steps will be taken. First, there will be a meeting with the angel to try to unite disorderly parties. This will take place at the Creator's discretion. A face to face confrontation will happen between God and Angel(s) to discuss the cause of this Angel's new development as well as come up with existing solutions for any issues that arise.

If no solution can be found, see Section IV, Note I

Section IV: MY KEYS NOW !

The keys to the Kingdom belong solely to the Creator of the Heavens. The keys to the Kingdom shall remain with God at all times. No angel shall have nor will be given the keys to the Kingdom unless first agreed upon by the Holy Trinity. Such instances are extreme and only to be decided as individual cases arise. An agreement between all God-parties will have one anonymous vote as to who is to receive the keys to the Kingdom besides the Almighty.

Note 1: If an angel is presently demonstrating action contrary to their anointed behavior and a solution is not found, the rule stands: there is no rebellion in Heaven. Safely monitor the being's present state and judge the condition of the being's heart towards Heaven and its Creator. If decided an action is deemed unlawful, the angel will suffer the consequence written in Note II.

If an angelic being also takes the keys to the Kingdom without being given the appropriate right from the Holy Trinity, the angel(s) will suffer the consequence written in Note II.

Note II: Any party who rebels to the above laws will face dire consequences. Any angel doomed to leave Heaven will be stripped from their title and position, never be allowed back in. A cursed option awaits them. These pre-mentioned parties will be cast out of Heaven after a honorable procession of five trumpets. After such procession, the rebellious parties will be driven out of Heaven. Forever.

God Almighty: _____
Signature

Jesus Christ: _____
Signature

Holy Spirit: _____
Signature

118

Thank you for reading! Sunshine would love to hear your review of this book! If you enjoyed it, tell her what you thought on Amazon.com or any other book retailer site! She loves hearing from her readers! If you need prayer for anything, let her know! She would love to pray for you!

Connect with Author Sunshine Rodgers:

SunshineRodgers.com

Facebook.com/SunshineRodgersBooks

Twitter: @Writer_Sunshine

Instagram: @AuthorSunshineRodgers

Follow Sunshine on Amazon.com and Goodreads!

I would love to thank Bill Vincent and the amazing editors, designers, and staff at RWG Publishing! Once again, you have made my dreams into a reality!

Thank you Evangelist Carl Harris for taking the time to write a foreword for this book. I loved bouncing ideas back and forth with you about the storyline and I appreciate you making sure my words were on point and as Biblically accurate as possible. You are someone I truly admire!

Thank you to my artist, Max Steele. Thank you for sharing your talent in this book! It truly livens up the pages!

I always have to say an endless thank you to my best friend, my husband and now my artist Travis Rodgers. Without your help and support, I would not be here today. Now, <u>both</u> of our names are on the front cover of a book!! Thank you for sharing your creativity! I cannot imagine life without you (nor would I ever want to!). Every part of me is in love with every part of you!

Thank you, God... for *you*, your inspiration and for essentially writing this book for me. You want your story to be heard.

- Sunshine Rodgers

Sunshine Rodgers has become a charismatic influence to this generation, writing about how good God is and how involved He is in our everyday lives. Her faith-based books create Heavenly perspectives never before imagined and shares a modern take on biblical stories. Her books include: *God the Father, Jesus the Big Brother, Holy Spirit the Best Friend* and *Last Night, When I Prayed, This is My Heaven* and *After You: A Demon is Always Lurking Nearby*. She spends her days traveling, attending author festivals, book signings, live interviews and speaking engagements. Sunshine's events and books have appeared in newspapers and literary magazines. She is a speaker and a motivator who has thousands of readers following her on social media and her personal blog.

Artists:

Travis Rodgers:

Travis is an Emmy nominated TV producer, voice-over artist, blogger, journalist, former professional wrestler and collector of many things. He's worked in TV and film for more than 15 years. And fun fact: he owns an official Red Ryder 200 shot range model air rifle!

Connect with Travis:

Twitter: @TravisBukowski

Blog: TravisBukowski.wordpress.com

YouTube: search Travis Bukowski

Instagram: @Travis Bukowski

Travis's illustrations: *animals, the forbidden tree, the GK logo, God and Adam, the planets, the sign, and the snake. He also is responsible for the signatures of the Trinity as well as the marks from Lucifer.*

Max Steele:

When Max was younger, he was always obsessed with animation; the way characters were designed, and the process behind making them stick out from the crowd. For as long as he can remember, he's been studying and illustrating characters and sketches. He was often told by peers and teachers that his "drawings were ridiculous," and that he "couldn't possibly make anything worth a passing glance" but thankfully Max wasn't a very good listener.

Connect with Max:

https://www.facebook.com/max.steele.98499

Max's designs: *Adam & Eve, the hands holding the keys (front cover design), his own portrait and Sunshine Rodgers' sketch*

Check other books by Sunshine Rodgers:

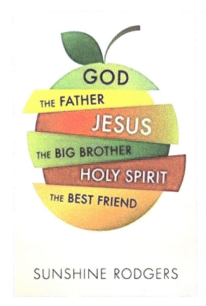

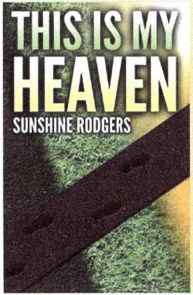

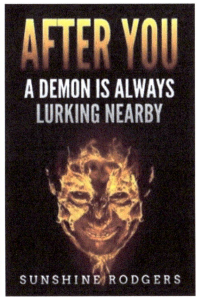

CPSIA information can be obtained
at www.ICGtesting.com
Printed in the USA
BVHW090959220519
548976BV00004B/44/P